TOSHIKI OKADA is a hugely admired playwright, director and novelist. Born in Yokohama in 1973, he formed the chelfitsch theatre company in 1997. Since then he has written and directed all of the company's productions, and has come to be known for his hyper-colloquial dialogue and staccato choreography. His play *Five Days in March*, on which the first story in *The End of the Moment We Had* is based, won the prestigious Kishida Kunio Drama Award. His works have been translated into many languages around the world.

SAM MALISSA has translated Japanese fiction and non-fiction, including work by Hideo Furukawa, Masatsugu Ono and Shun Medoruma. He has a master's degree in Japanese literature from Yale University.

PUSHKIN PRESS

TOSHIKI OKADA

THE END
OF THE
MOMENT
WE HAD

translated by
SAM MALISSA

PUSHKIN PRESS

SERIES EDITORS: David Karashima and Michael Emmerich
TRANSLATION EDITOR: Elmer Luke

Pushkin Press
71–75 Shelton Street
London WC2H 9JQ

The End of the Moment We Had was first published as
Watashitachi ni yurusareta tokubetsu na jikan no owari in Japan, 2007

First published by Pushkin Press in 2018

The publisher gratefully acknowledges the support of the
British Centre for Literary Translation and the Nippon Foundation

1 3 5 7 9 8 6 4 2

ISBN 13: 978 1 78227 416 2

Designed and typeset in Marbach by Tetragon, London

Printed and bound by CPI Group (UK) Ltd, Croydon, CR0 4YY

www.pushkinpress.com

CONTENTS

THE END OF THE MOMENT WE HAD

7

MY PLACE IN PLURAL

63

THE END OF THE
MOMENT WE HAD

THE SIX OF THEM were in a clump, talking loudly, relentlessly, sometimes shouting, from the moment they stepped into the last car of the Hibiya Line metro. They carried on, leaning against the glass of the conductor's booth, sliding their backs along the lateral bar. You'd think they were trying to drown out the rumble and screech of the train. But no one on the train there with them was thinking that. They were stuck with these guys. They couldn't escape the shouting. Robbed of their solitude, they stared at the screens of their phones, or at the ads, or at the floor. No one said a word. Some maybe were thinking, these guys will get off at Roppongi, so it won't be much longer. Which was what happened.

The six guys were drunk, but it wasn't until they got to Roppongi that they realized how drunk they were. The doors opened, they were sucked out, and they were still shouting. It wasn't one conversation, each was talking with whoever happened to be nearest them, so Minobe with Suzuki, Azuma with Yukio, Yasui with Ishihara. But more or less they were a group. All drunk. They were louder than anyone else around, but they didn't notice nor care, or maybe it was their intention to be loud. As they climbed the stairs to the exit, they never once lowered their voices. At the wicket they lined up behind one another, as if it were a ritual, to pass through the same gate, shouting the whole time. Ishihara was the last in line, and when he fumbled through his pockets and couldn't find his ticket, he yelled out to Yasui, who was in front of him and at that instant about to pass through the barrier. Yasui stopped in his tracks, and Ishihara pressed up behind him, crotch to ass, and the two tried to pass through the barrier as one. The sensor went off, beeping its high pitch, and the flaps of the electronic barrier slammed shut on them. No problem. Yasui and Ishihara busted through with the full force of their drunkenness and fell forwards onto the ground. The others were right there watching, howling with laughter, loud as ever.

Moving in a mass, they made their way above ground, where, afraid they wouldn't be able to hear each other, they raised their voices even more. At one point they must have figured they could turn it down a notch and still be heard. Even so, definitely, they were loud. As they headed towards their destination—the SuperDeluxe club-slash-event space—their voices made it to the other side of the street and bounced back, even through the clamour of Roppongi Drive. The endless flow of cars and exhausts, and on top of that a jumble of noise. Clamour: it gets caught up in an invisible whorl, gets warmed by night air and starts to rise, rise until it's looking down over the whole scene, the dots of light blurring as they grow more distant, bleeding into each other until they look like thick haze hanging heavily over the ground.

When Yasui was little, he had gone up to the observation deck of Tokyo Tower and been startled by how all the cars below seemed like toys. It had been during the day, but the night laid itself over this memory and he now saw the buzz of Roppongi from a bird's-eye view. He was at the back of the group, rubbing his thigh where the flaps of the ticket barrier had slammed into him. A bruise was forming, but he didn't know that yet. He and Ishihara—trashed, semi-conscious, words tumbling out of their mouths—were going on about girls. Ishihara's eyes were glazed over. When Yasui asked Ishihara *where are we going again?*, Ishihara didn't answer, maybe because the question didn't register. So Yasui just followed along. It wasn't really clear that anybody knew where they were going, though it appeared they were going *somewhere*.

There wasn't a moment when one of them wasn't shouting. The configuration of the group was constantly changing, like when Minobe and Suzuki turned around to stare at the girl who'd just passed, saying something at high volume about her legs—really just the back of her knees—and Azuma and Yukio brushed by them and ended up at the front of the pack. And then Minobe, who had been talking with Suzuki, suddenly yelled something to Azuma and Yukio about the girl, and Azuma yelled something back. Yasui tried to catch what they were saying but didn't quite get it, because he'd been in the middle of a sentence talking to Ishihara, and Suzuki was basically shouting stuff to himself. You get the picture: a mash of meaningless noise.

When they stumbled into SuperDeluxe, the eight-o'clock performance was still waiting to start. But they almost didn't get to the place at all. The sign for SuperDeluxe was small and not easy to see if you're not looking for it, and the six of them were talking (or shouting) away, paying no mind to anything. They were almost down the slope of the hill, when Azuma, regaining awareness, noticed that the Nishi-Azabu intersection was up ahead, growing larger as they got closer, and wondered if they'd gone too far. He kind of mumbled it to himself, which no one heard, and they all kept going. Finally, Azuma was totally sure they were way past where they were supposed to go, so he stopped, and said loudly, loudly enough so the other five stopped to listen, *hey, I think we like went too far*. But even though he was shouting, it still somehow sounded like he was talking to himself. He looked over his shoulder, up the hill. Then he turned his whole body around and started back the way they came. The others didn't say anything, they turned and followed. Just like that. They were paying much more attention now, and this time they spotted the sign for SuperDeluxe, which was so nondescript that the six of them started moaning loudly about it, before pushing open the door to the place and spilling inside.

It was a wide room with a low ceiling, which made the space feel flat. Low tables were set up randomly, surrounded by sofas and chairs of different shapes and materials. The furniture was purplish and yellowish, although it was hard to say for sure because the space was dark and the lighting was tinted. Some of the seats were covered with shag. There were stools with pink reptile-skin covers, and big plastic things that weren't quite sofas or benches but had curves that made them look warped. Almost all the seats were taken. Along the farthest wall was the stage, which was painted white and had mic stands and guitars and amps and chairs, and a tangle of cords snaking between them. Right in front of the stage was the only open spot, a low table and exactly six chairs, which Yasui saw and hurried to claim. The others followed. They dropped their stuff and made their way to the bar. They ordered individually and paid for their own drinks. They all got beer.

SuperDeluxe was supposed to have some kind of performance that night, but five of the six guys didn't know that. They had just come as a drunken mass. They didn't know what was supposed to happen, a performance or whatever, or even that the place they were in held performances. The only one who knew anything was Azuma. He had heard about the performance from a girl he'd met at the movies a couple of days before. She'd said she was nineteen. It was a small movie theatre in Shibuya, open only a few years, the upholstery on the seats still smelling like a clothing store.

*

She looked nineteen, for sure. On account of her skin. But her face was busted. It was like she knew better than anyone how busted her face was, and that made her extra-friendly, and you could see that in her face too, which only made it worse. It was all smushed and embarrassed-like, hard to look at. There were plenty of empty seats in the movie theatre, as always, but there I was, watching the movie with her sitting next to me, on my left. For the whole movie I tried to make my left side cold and unwelcoming. When it was over, the left half of my body was numb. That numbness went away, but it feels like it's still there, waiting just under my skin. As soon as we got into SuperDeluxe, I started wondering if she was here. I looked around the room a bunch of times. The room, everything between the concrete walls and the floor, felt kind of soft, because of the pulse of all the people, the smell of everything, and the music and the lights. I prayed I wouldn't spot her, but I kept looking for her.

How I met this girl: A couple of days ago I pre-bought two tickets to a movie, one was for this other girl I was seeing—I guess she was my girlfriend, what-ever—but then she texted me that she couldn't make it, and I was like that's cool. I figured I could sell her ticket, no problem. Some days in March are warm and some are cold, and it was cold that day, but I waited outside the theatre to catch someone who was otherwise going to pay full price at the box office. A guy showed up first, so I didn't offer. Next was another guy. Then several more guys, and guys with girls, so I just looked upwards. Near the top of a building, there was a square electronic billboard, like it was floating in the sky, playing through a loop of ads over and over and over. Then, finally, a girl came by. That was her. I might have been pickier, but I guess I was worried that she was my last chance. She was pretty chunky, like she snacked all the time or something, and the way she walked was like sad and apologetic. But I said hi anyway. She came over, and she bought the ticket, and we were standing there, and I started regretting the whole thing right then. We went down the stairs together, and she started asking questions: *Do you go to the movies a lot? What kind of movies do you like? Why do you like that kind of movie? Do you go to a movie because who's in it or who directed it?* I was hoping to escape and went and took a seat in the middle of a row, but she hustled after me, fast for someone her size—I swear, I felt the air shake with her mass—and she dropped herself into the seat next to me. The questioning didn't stop: *So when you like a movie, they release the soundtrack, right, are you the type who buys the soundtrack?* She would have kept going with the interrogation, but the lights began to dim. Commercials and trailers, one after the next after the next, taking forever like usual. Finally the movie started. It was a Canadian movie, about four teenage girls, and they each go through stereotypical teenage experiences. The plot didn't make a big deal of itself, but there didn't seem to be anything like structure either, everything just happened randomly. I got bored partway through and pretty much gave up on watching it. Instead I just sat there listening to the English that I didn't understand and telling myself what a fool I was, waiting to sell my extra ticket to some girl and getting what I deserved. I played the whole scene over and over again in my head—spotting her and, for some crazy reason, saying hi—and actually it felt way more real than anything happening on the movie screen. Then the movie ended.

As soon as the lights came on, she started talking again. *Umm, what did you think of it? It was pretty good, right? Maybe not so good? If you ask me, I guess I think it was like great. You know there was that one black actress? And the guy who played her older brother? I heard he's like in a theatre group, like it's his theatre group, or a performance group, one of those, you know? I'm not just telling you to show that I know stuff, I'm more like, wow, he really knows what he's doing as an actor, that's what I meant. What did you think about him? Don't you think he's good? And like, oh right, I heard a rumour he's going to be in a performance, the day after tomorrow or something, at a place in Roppongi, I mean it's not a rumour, it's like true, I just for some reason said it was a rumour, and like they never perform in theatres, they always do it in like clubs or bars and stuff, their show, or I guess their performance, they're like performers, but they don't use a stage set or anything, they just like get a mic and improvise, something like that, yeah.*

When I told the guy about this performance, he said, *maybe I'll go.* I know he was just saying that, but I forced myself, I went out of my way to believe him, so I just came out and said, *oh really, then why don't we go together.* I did it because I didn't want to think he was just saying he'd go, and because if he wasn't just saying it, I wanted to see if things could go farther, and because some small part of me really thought he wanted to go. I knew exactly what would happen if I said, *why don't we go together,* but I said it anyway, because like if I had a positive attitude and gave it a shot, it would happen, so I came out and said it as sincerely as I could. I said it all brightly, to cheer myself on. Even if he saw right through to my trembling little ulterior motive—though I don't think it was anything sinister like ulterior, I think it was sweet and kind of innocent—even if he saw through me, I told myself I didn't care. Which of course was a lie, if he saw through me I'd just want to die. When I was about to say, *why don't we go together*, I thought that as soon as I finished saying it, I should stare into his eyes as hard as I could. So I did. I knew that he might get put off by me giving him that kind of look, but I did it anyway. Then when I was staring into his eyes, I knew that I had to really plead with my eyes or it wouldn't work, and I didn't let myself think it wouldn't work because it was my eyes, in my face. If I looked away quickly because I knew it was putting him off, that would be even worse, and I mean I knew right away that even if I stared into his eyes, nothing was going to happen, but I forced myself to stare into his eyes for a while— a really short while, maybe just a few seconds. But it wasn't working, like I knew it wouldn't, and I gave up. For a moment I didn't know where I should look next, which was how I ended up looking hard at the wall. It was like throwing a lump of clay against the wall as hard as I could and it was just sticking there. A light grey spot, hardly noticeable, but it leaves a stain that never comes out, and even though it's basically totally meaningless, there it is forever, so that's what I decided to stare at. I tried to make it mean something by looking at it, even though it didn't want to be given any meaning.

To be honest, by that point in time I was totally sick of myself. But I was telling myself that I always get sick of myself too quickly. The lobby of the movie theatre had posted these magazine articles about the movies they were showing. The two of us were standing there, me kind of leaning against the wall, kind of like talking. Maybe fifty centimetres above my right shoulder there was on the wall this cut-out little article from a magazine I know the name of but have never read. From where he was standing, my head was in the way of him seeing the article, not that he was trying to see it, he was probably just thinking about getting out of there. I leant against the wall all heavy, like I couldn't move if I wanted to, so he felt like he couldn't just leave me there. I made him feel that way. Of course he knew I was just putting it on. But all he could do was stand there. He didn't lean against the wall like I did, he just stood there. He stood there for a whole hour, until his feet ached.

The two of us were talking about something, but there was suddenly a break in the conversation, like a gap between us. I remembered that before the movie started we were talking about soundtracks, but the movie started and the conversation got cut off, so I thought I would bring that back up again, and I did. *Umm, I've actually been wondering something this whole time, so, before the movie started, we were talking about this, right? I mean I just wanted to go back to that, you know? So like are you the type who buys soundtracks of movies you like? That's what I asked before, remember, and you said you're not a soundtrack buyer, right? And then I was like, why not? And that's when the movie started, I mean it was just the trailers, but we couldn't really talk any more, so that's where the conversation ended, right? You remember all that, right? So can we pick up where we left off?* And when I asked that, he said *sure.* So I did. *So when you say you don't buy soundtracks, why is that? To be honest, I am really curious, like do you have a reason?* When I was asking him this, I leant even more of my body weight against the wall. I wanted him to lean on the wall too, so we could be leaning the same way on the same wall, except that he was going to be facing me and talking to me, so I was like inviting him to join me. But not surprisingly, he didn't lean. Though I have to say it was a pretty subtle invitation. I knew it probably didn't even get through to him.

So he said, *yeah, when it comes to soundtracks, sometimes I want to buy it right after I've seen the movie, and especially if it's like a good movie, or like if the music made a strong impression, so sometimes I feel like I have to buy it*—and I said, *uh huh, yeah.* He kept going, *so, yeah, I get it, sure, but you know, every time I go and buy one, and I've bought a bunch, it's always like, I mean I'm saying this from experience here, because I've bought a whole bunch, but don't you always just get tired of the soundtrack like almost right away? No? Maybe you don't, but I do, you know, and at some point I realized that, and I was like, okay, from now on, no more soundtracks for me, so I stopped.* He was still standing there, not leaning on the wall. I thought what he was saying was so right on. I mean, I was pretty impressed. *Yeah, I totally get what you're saying,* I said, *I mean totally!* And then I felt like I was kind of floating. I got nervous, I had to say something, so I blurted out, *I guess I should stop buying soundtracks too.* But as soon as I said it, that floating sensation got worse, I didn't feel like I had got any-where. All he said was, *it's whatever you want, buy 'em or don't.* And I said, *oh, right, you're so right.* And I kept going, *basically everyone's got their preferences—or, you know, not preferences, but you know what I mean—and so like everyone's different, right? So everyone can buy them if they want or not buy them if they don't, is what you're saying, right?* He said, *sure.* Oh god, I was so unbeliev-ably stupid, when I said, *I guess I should stop buying soundtracks too,* I mean what kind of a statement is that,

I have no clue—I should just shut my mouth and die. But even if it was a statement, the response is obvious, so saying something like that like it's a statement, I mean it was so lame, but I said it, and thinking about myself saying it, I was like *oh my god, I'm the worst, my life is over*, and I actually said that out loud, which I didn't even realize until after I said it, I'm so stupid I should just die, and he must have been thinking the exact same thing. When he heard me say *my life is over*, he made a confused face, or I'm pretty sure he did. But he wasn't making that face to be mean or anything, it just happened, which actually made it hurt even worse, and I had no idea what to do next. I never know what to do next. I'm always about to fall apart, which I guess is selfish of me, or weak. I couldn't stop thinking about our soundtrack conversation when I said, *I guess I should stop buying soundtracks too* and he said, *it's whatever you want*. But what he really meant to say was *make up your own fuckin' mind, moron*. And I finally realized it, I mean I only just realized—too late—but that's what it was. It took me this long to understand that I really am a moron. I felt humiliated, even though it was too late to do anything about it, and my body started getting all hot. But maybe I was getting hot from something besides humiliation, maybe something a little different, but I'm a moron, so I don't really know what else it could be. But either way, I was getting hot, and I felt like I needed to say something, and I ended up saying something totally stupid. *Today's like my lucky day, I'm the worst at getting tickets, I know I should have pre-brought a ticket 'cause it's cheaper that way but I didn't, but I mean because of, you know, I got my ticket for cheaper so I totally got lucky, really. So I really, I want to say thanks*—and then I took the quickest little breath, like as if I was swimming, and I kept going. *But I know if there was an extra ticket, that means that there was supposed to be someone else (with you), so like, sorry, um, if it's no big deal, and I mean if it is, then don't worry about it, but I'd like to know (your) name, first name only would be okay, or like a nickname, but I just want to know what I can call (you).* By that point I was barely keeping it together. By the way, about the (you) (in parentheses), that's because I wanted to say it out loud but couldn't even do that. Before I knew what I was doing, I told him he could call me Miffy, which is my screen name, and it's so lame I've never actually told it to anyone who I know in real life, but I went and told him. I wasn't sure any more if I was saying the words I was thinking, if they were coming out of my mouth and he heard them, or if they were all still in my head, unsaid, which meant they never reached him and I just wanted to say them, I couldn't tell. My body was still feeling hot, but it was like I didn't know which part of my body felt hot. And I just kept talking. I had to find out his name. If I didn't, then I would be totally worthless. That terrified me. The heat in my body made me feel like I was somehow outside the moment I was living in. That made me get reckless, and want to stay that way, so I really went for it. *Sorry, um, I just want to ask again, it totally doesn't have to be a real name, just anything, like a screen name would be fine, I just wanna know,* what should I call (you)? *is what's on my mind, I mean, I've just really been wondering, I mean, wanting to ask, so, like, I'm asking now, um.* That's what I said to him. But in the end he never told me his name. He didn't lie or make up a screen name, he just ignored the question, so even though I tried, it didn't mean anything, which was like the worst. In the hour or so since the movie ended, how many stupid mistakes had I made? It'd be like counting stars, and I didn't feel like counting. If I tried, I would just feel worse and worse, I'd probably want to die, so I didn't. I thought that my body was getting hotter because it didn't want to live any more. I knew I was losing him. I knew he wasn't actually listening to anything I was saying, that he wouldn't remember any of it. But he felt like he couldn't just ditch me, so he stood there pretending to listen, zoning out, thinking about whatever. Like what would be the funniest song to play over this pathetic situation, or something like that. Normally that would embarrass me to death, but I was already torturing myself plenty, so getting ignored wasn't anything I was worrying about. He was saying something to me. At that moment I didn't have the energy to understand him. But I could get the idea, he was making moves to leave, and sure enough he made a little apologetic face and right away said goodbye and walked off, footsteps hurrying towards the movie theatre exit. When I was completely out of sight, he slowed down, then looked over his shoulder to make sure I wasn't like stalking him. Then he called his girlfriend, the one who was supposed to go to the movies with him, and told her the movie was shit, he slept through half of it. They talked about other stuff, then made plans to meet up, and he got on a different subway from the one he would usually take to go home.

The performance started. The mood in the room shifted with almost no warning, like an ambush. Or maybe it just felt that way to the guys because we were all drunk and had no concept of time. There was a change in the quality of quiet, like when snow suddenly stops falling. The murmurs of the crowd died down, and the house lights dimmed a little—not that they had been very bright to begin with. So maybe it was just the impression of the lights dimming. The six of us were all still drinking beer, to the point where none of us knew how many we'd had. Everyone finished the little bit that remained in our paper cups—it seemed like the thing to do with the lights going down and the feeling that the show was about to start, and after a bit the performers came out. There was nothing flashy about it, neither their entrance nor the performance that followed, it had a totally relaxed feel. First, a white girl took the mic. She wound the cord a few times, which there didn't seem to be any reason for doing other than to mark time. She started talking in English. Next to her stood a Japanese girl who was interpreting, and she had a mic in her hand too. The white girl spoke in a rich voice, sometimes suddenly getting louder, and the first couple of times she raised her voice it triggered a screech of feedback, but the feedback stopped quickly enough. She was explaining what the performance was going to be about. Although the explanation was already part of the performance. *We'll be talking about things, but we don't know what we'll be talking about, and the reason why not is that we haven't prepared anything. But we'll talk anyway.* That must have been what she said, because that's what the interpreter interpreted after her. *There aren't just mics on the stage,* she said, *there's also a mic on a stand in the audience, and it's open to anyone who wants to speak.* The audience mic stood right behind where the six of us were sitting, kind of blocking the aisle. *If anyone has anything they want to say, feel free to get on the mic at any time.* The interpreter said all that in Japanese. Of course nobody got up and went to the mic. The room fell silent. This is, after all, Japan. The girl, and I'm just guessing here, she let the silence go on, thinking maybe that would get past the Japan-ness. But before the silence could get too heavy it was broken. One of the performers, the young black guy who might have been in the movie I saw, walked over to the audience mic and started telling his story. He had dreads, but they didn't make his head look that much bigger and they weren't flashy or intimidating, if anything they made him look sophisticated. His story didn't last long. *When I was sixteen I got my first ever job. A janitor in a Dunkin' Donuts. At the end of my first day, the manager called me into the office and asked, how do you like the job? But I didn't answer.* That was the end of the story. He stepped away from the mic, opened one of the folding chairs onstage and sat down. Silence returned to the room. It lasted a lot longer than the first time. At first everyone thought it would end right away, that someone else would stand up and go to the mic and pick up where the first performer left off. But no one did, and the silence stretched on much longer than anyone thought it would. It must have been part of the performance, an intentional silence. It went on and on, to the point where the least secure people in the audience must have been squirming under the weight of the silence, when finally the girl sitting next to the black guy on the stage made a move like she was going to stand up, and then she actually did stand up, took the mic and started talking. It was just when people were starting to think that the silence had gone on for too long, just as they were facing the need to decide what they were prepared to do about it. Thanks to the girl standing up, everything taking shape in their minds settled back, only half-formed. All their discomfort was neutralized along with everything else they were feeling, then it vanished, as if it had never been there at all.

This is what the girl said: She was staying at a hotel in Shibuya. That morning she went out for a walk and she happened upon a protest march. It was a few days before the US began their invasion of Iraq. The protest was against the war. She joined in and marched with them. She was surprised at how narrow the column of the marchers was in Japan compared to the protests she had seen elsewhere, and how orderly the police were, escorting the marchers. She heard music that was probably from a portable CD player somewhere in the march, and then somebody handed her a tambourine. That was the end of her story, and the girl sat down. This time there was only a short pause. Then the girl who spoke first stepped up and said something very brief. The immediate Japanese translation told us that the mic was open to all of us. Then another silence. Another long one.

I wondered what I would say if I went to the mic, tried to picture myself doing it. After a little while a man stood up, but at first I didn't notice him. It wasn't until he got right up to the mic that I did. He was middle-aged, with greying hair and rimless glasses, and he had a mellow vibe. We watched to see what he would do. I asked myself if I would get up too, all six of us did, I mean only vaguely, but we did. He said that he found out about this event online. He got on a plane from Kyushu to Tokyo to come see it. *I have grave apprehensions about the war that's about to begin,* he said. *When I was young it was the war in Vietnam. Back then, there were bands like Peter, Paul and Mary, and we all sang their songs together. But now there are no songs like that.* That was when he lost my interest. Is this old guy going to keep talking? I wondered, but that was all he had to say. While he shared his thoughts, the interpreter spoke in a low voice to the performers, telling them in English what the guy said. One of them nodded repeatedly. The man at the mic stood there for another minute even though he had stopped talking, like it took him some time to realize that he was done. When he finally came back to himself, he stepped out of the light into the shadows and went back to his seat. Then he raised his glass from the table to his lips and steadied himself. None of us paid any more attention to him. No one else made any moves towards the mic and the room got silent again. The air was still; you could hear the bubbles in the beer. This went on for a while, the echoes or maybe more like the reverberations of what we'd just heard hanging over the room like smoke. But it wasn't exactly a vibe relating to what the man had said, if anything it was resistance, annoyance even, except that's probably not quite right, it was both, a feel in the room that was kind of obviously a combination of resistance and agreement, and I was glad, because that was how I felt too. I wanted to try to put a name to the feel at that moment, like if it existed independently from all the bodies in the room—I mean if someone was observing, from a distance, what would they call that feeling. I considered really thinking about it, but I didn't do it. I wanted another beer, but

I couldn't get up in the middle of this and go to the bar. I turned to look at the bar anyway, see how far away it was. My eyes swept over the audience, and that was when I spotted a girl, who looked back at me. She wasn't the girl from the movie theatre. After the performance ended, she and I stood by the bar talking. Then we took a taxi to Shibuya and got a room at a love hotel. It wasn't a Friday or Saturday so even though we got there pretty late, we had no problem getting a room.

One of the other audience members who got up in front of the mic during the performance—after a while lots of people got up to say something—was a girl who started off by saying she was an interpreter. By the time she was on the mic, the performance was winding down, and the whole room was full of everyone's desire for the thing to finish. But she just talked on, nonchalant-like. Or maybe she really couldn't read the room.

So I also work as an interpreter—she seemed to be speaking to the Japanese woman interpreting on stage—*and as far as what exactly an interpreter does, well, I guess you all know this, but basically they take what someone's said, in my case I work from English, so I take what someone's said in English and translate it into Japanese, or the other way around, so I take what's been said, I mean what's been said by someone besides me, and translate it and communicate it and that's the job of an interpreter, right? So tonight I've been watching all kinds of people get up and say something on the mic, and like I thought for a change it might be interesting to translate what I myself was thinking. So now I'm gonna take what's on my mind and translate it into English. Is that all right?* She didn't really mean it as a question, and she wasn't expecting anyone to answer. So she went on. *But now I'm like, do I even have anything to say? Which makes me start to think that maybe I don't, and I guess my only realizing that now that I'm up here has some of you wondering like what's with this girl, right? But you know, I guess I really don't have anything to say. I mean, I'm an interpreter, so I can speak, or like, you know, understand English, so being here tonight and listening to everyone go back and forth really made me feel like I wanted to give my opinion too, but I guess at like the moment of truth I realized that I don't even have an opinion. Sorry about that. Really, there's got to be something, um, oh hey I know, so I saw* Bowling for Columbine *too. I can talk about that, you know, it was really chilling, I was like, whoa, this is how the media gets us all worked up and makes fear take root inside of us, you know? I saw it at the theatre in Ebisu, it was super-crowded. And I mean I think it's great that so many people went to see a movie like that.*

The girl I went to the hotel with wasn't this girl on the mic, it was her friend. They came to the performance together. I noticed this girl actively watching her friend get all excited on the mic, and I stared at her. It was a few moments before she turned to look back at me. The first thing that made me like her was how her fringe hung in a diagonal line across her forehead. I think she must have cut them herself. But I never asked her about it. When I was looking at her before she looked back, I tried to guess the odds of her getting up on the mic, like I was placing a bet. In the end she didn't. Her friend did, but she didn't. Although I wonder how many people were actually still listening. A lot of people had already talked. Between the time that had passed since the performance started and all the alcohol consumed by all the people who had been sitting there the whole time, the atmosphere was starting to get thick. I was busy paying attention to the fringe of the girl who wasn't the interpreter. And there were also fragments of what some people had said at the mic sticking in my head, like pricking me. Like there was this one girl—*I saw the protest march today too, and I thought about joining in, but in the end I couldn't bring myself to.* And there was a guy who before the interpreter girl talked about having seen *Bowling for Columbine* went up and said he'd seen it and what he thought about it. There were others. But by that point in the night I was done listening. I wanted to have sex with the girl with the fringe. I was past listening. Since we got to SuperDeluxe, I had two or maybe more than two beers, and together with what I drank before, it was some stupid amount. The six of us had been drinking all night. My eyes felt all bleary. They probably looked that way to her too, when our eyes met, but that was probably for the best—I mean I'm just guessing here—rather than me trying to act cool I was able to just stare right at her, which must have made an impression. Normally, when I'm not drunk, my mind wants to jump from whatever I'm doing to the next thing, and you can see it in my eyes. My eyes are always darting around. But when I drink, the more faded I get, the more I can pay attention to whatever I'm looking at. My eyes stay put, I don't need to worry about them doing their own thing. They just stay where they are. I thought about how the one performer who went to the protest said she was impressed with how tight and narrow the marching column was. Come to think of it, the marches in America and Europe I saw on the news took up the entire street. I thought about that for a bit. As I did, my eyes started to lose focus, my vision got blurry, but the performance continued, didn't matter how drunk I was or what I was thinking or what my eyes were doing. The performers started shouting questions from the stage, and the audience was supposed to answer yes or no. There must've been ten questions they shouted. But now I can only remember one, which was the last one. *Is Bush bad?* There was a louder response than for any of the earlier questions, and people shouted from here and there, from everywhere really, the whole audience was shouting, *yes! yes! yes! yes!* But at the end, overlapping with the last cries of *yes!*—strictly speaking, a tiny bit after—was a single loud *no!* It was a man's voice. Of course all the performers looked towards where the voice came from. They could tell right away who had said it. One of the performers said they wanted to hear what the man had to say, then the interpreter translated the request. The man approached the mic. He walked like he was trying to avoid looking sheepish but also didn't want to seem too eager. Whatever was on his mind as he walked to the mic stand, it took him a few moments to get there. Then he spoke to the crowd that had been waiting to hear what he was going to say: *So, I'm guessing I was called out because you want to know why I said no*—and here he smiled in a way that could be read as either natural or unnatural. He seemed to be wanting to give off a casual feel. He continued speaking, his smile still lingering. *So, the reason is pretty simple, basically, everyone here said yes, which feels a little creepy, and that was my main reason. I don't like Bush from a standpoint of policy or anything like that. Rather than thinking about whether or not my answer is actually no, I just felt like at least one person had to say no, otherwise we'd have everybody here saying yes and that doesn't feel right, it actually feels a little dangerous. That was really it.* The interpreter put all of that into English. While she was doing her thing, the man kept smiling. As if reacting to that, the interpreter had a little smile on her face too as she spoke in English. After a brief silence, the black guy who told the story about Dunkin' Donuts nodded forcefully. He kept nodding and said that if he was watching the performance as an audience member, he probably would have said no for the same reason. The interpreter said that in Japanese. That was the end of that interaction. After that a few more people got up and said things. Up on stage, the performers talked more, in response to the comments from the audience, or not. Every so often through the night the performers played some terrible covers. The guitars, the keyboards, the drums, the vocals, it was all awful. But it didn't really matter. Some of the songs they played were originals. Those were awful too. After each one someone else would get up and say something and someone would respond.

Speaking, music, repeat. As the performance went on, never deviating from that pattern, it became easier for people to go up to the mic and speak. But at the same time the audience was growing tired of the repetition, bit by bit but plain enough to see. Then it got to the point where most of the audience was starting to feel that this loose performance, loose in both the good and the bad sense, would soon come to an end. I felt it too. By that point I was already feeling like I wasn't in Japan. The girl and I took that feeling to the hotel, where we spent the next four days with it. Several times we tried to figure out where the feeling came from. But we never came up with anything that seemed right. It couldn't have been just because the performers were foreigners. Nearly everything the performers talked about had to do with the war that was about to start. The clock was ticking down on the ultimatum Bush gave Iraq, and the whole world was paying attention, all they could do was watch and wait. Everyone knew what was going to happen, but it hadn't happened yet. The performance took place in the middle of all this. So it was obvious that one of the aims of the performance was to spark a debate about what was happening. And sure enough some people went to the mic and said what they had to say about it, while others stood up without having anything particular in mind, *Sorry,* they said, *I don't really have anything to say but I just kind of came up to the microphone anyway*, then they shrugged and waddled back to their seat.

When we were at the hotel, our conversation kept going back to the performance—*by the time that interpreter girl went up to the mic, everyone had pretty much had it, I doubt anyone was actually listening to her, which kind of sucks*—is what I said, and so she was like, *yeah, but you know she's always, I mean she never really pays attention to the vibe, or it's like whatever the feel is, it has nothing to do with her, it's basically always that way with her.*

We picked the hotel at random, and the room was pretty cheaply put together, but that was fine. At first I thought the wallpaper was old and grimy, and it was only later that I realized it was just pink wallpaper. She let her thick hair down, so the diagonal line of her fringe was gone. Without that she had a different feel, maybe less subdued. I noticed that her eyes angled up at the corners. The conversation trailed off, maybe we weren't done talking but there was a break, and we nuzzled in close again, started taking little nips and nibbles at each other, getting back into it.

We stayed for four nights, and on the morning of the fifth day we said goodbye. Only once did we venture out into Shibuya. Otherwise we were holed up in the room the entire time. There was a TV, but we never turned it on. We had no idea what was going on in the outside world, not even the weather. In between sessions of sex we talked, like everyone does, about all kinds of things. I can't remember everything we talked about. We never told each other our names or phone numbers or email addresses. Pretty much nothing about ourselves, none of the usual stuff you'd chat about, like where you work, or how you hate the people you work with—none of that. Instead we talked about when we were little. Why is it that when you're all spent after sex you want to talk about your childhood, especially when you don't know anything about the other person? I don't think either one of us knew whether we were intentionally avoiding talking about ourselves in the present or whether it just happened. But I think some part of us knew that this was the best thing to do. Like maybe your childhood self is your truest self, but that actually isn't true at all, so stories from your childhood are convenient that way. I've used them to get through casual sex encounters with girls before, and I did it this time too.

We talked in bed. The sheets had that impersonal feel that love hotel beds always have, I could feel it on my back, under the palms of my hands. They were brittle with starch to show they'd been washed, and they gave off this disgust, this contempt for the act of human beings fucking. They didn't try to hide how much they loathed us. They wanted to make sure we knew. So I figured, well, this bed isn't for sleeping by yourself, there'll always be another person, so it doesn't matter all that much if the sheets aren't like saying *welcome, how nice to have you here*, and then I felt like my mind was being read, like I was being seen through. But by who? By the hotel staff. And by the sheets themselves. I was sure of it. I moved my hands to her skin, and her skin was warm. We talked about our childhoods. We tried talking about music but it was immediately clear that we didn't like any of the same stuff so we just let that topic be. Movies and manga were easier. Like I said, we never talked about ourselves, I mean our real selves, and it was almost like we had at some point agreed on that as a rule, which felt like a miracle. I also knew that under no circumstances could I talk about this miracle. It sounds stupid, but I was scared that if I went and said it then something would change. The rule had to be followed at all costs, I mean it felt that way to me, and maybe to her too. And we did, we followed the rule, for the whole time we were together. Even when we weren't talking about ourselves, there was enough to talk about. Like the performance, we talked a lot about that. We never got tired of talking about that. Whenever we got to something we couldn't figure out, we would just have sex again. Neither one of us spoke in a hurry, so the conversation had a nice, relaxed pace. As we got used to each other the pace picked up a little, but it stayed easy. It was like that for the whole time, from when we first went to the hotel. Even going to the hotel just kind of happened, same as the boundaries of what we were going to talk about, without either of us outright suggesting it.

We were lying side by side on top of the sheets, which were all twisted up from the last round of sex. I said to her, *I'm really bad at English, so I can't say for sure, but I thought that performance, you know, this might just be me, but I thought that performance was pretty great, you know?* and I genuinely meant it. I had the feeling that the experience was going to stay with me for the rest of my life. It could just be the afterglow from sex, but I really wanted to communicate to her how honestly excited I was about the performance.

Although I might have told her that in the taxi on the way to the hotel, or it may have been that we were already talking about it when we first met at SuperDeluxe. The performance was staying with me like the lingering heat on your skin after spending a day at the beach, warmth that you feel into the night. The show was over and the lights were back on. The area around the bar was a little brighter than the rest of the room, and we stood there talking. It only took a couple minutes of conversation to make up our minds. We left the place and went straight to the hotel. I didn't say much to the five guys I had come with. I just went back to where they were all sitting, grabbed my stuff, must have said something about what I was doing, and that was that. The girl and I caught a taxi as soon as we stepped outside. Sitting in the back seat, holding hands like lovers, we headed to Shibuya.

The performance made it feel like we were in another country, I said to her, *and I don't think it was just because the performers were foreigners.* I whispered that to her or something like it, maybe not fully whispering but anyway in a quiet voice, my mouth close to her ear. But I was also completely wasted, so I probably didn't manage to say any of that in a logical and intelligible way—even when I'm sober I'm not the best at communicating stuff like that—so the best I could do was to try over and over again, tracing the same line of conversation, and even then I doubt I managed to get it quite right. She was skinny, and her fingers and the palm of her hand didn't have much meat on them. The feel of her fingers laced between mine actually hurt a little, the bony sharpness of them, it was like they existed to give that pain, and that pain felt kind of good. I wiggled my fingers between hers like to appreciate it. We pretended the driver couldn't see us. He probably knew what was going on, but he was an older guy who was good at acting like nothing was happening in his taxi, and if he did suspect something, he knew better than to make too big of a show ignoring it, since that would just tip us off to the fact that he knew, but anyway even if he did know I really didn't care. He must have seen us making out in the rear-view mirror. My other hand was up her skirt, not quite in her panties but rubbing the top of her thighs through her stockings as voices kept going back and forth on the taxi radio. And still I couldn't get away from thinking how at SuperDeluxe, when the audience members went up to the mic, they were speaking in Japanese, but it almost sounded like English, and why did it sound that way? I went back and forth over these thoughts, running my hands over her stockings, imagining the feel of the bare skin underneath. Although, I mean, I couldn't be too obvious about rubbing her thighs, so a lot of the time I just had my hand on her thigh, resting. Now I wonder what she was thinking after hearing me say what I said about the performance, or if she even heard it at all. When I said what I said, how come she didn't answer? Did she try to say something, or try to get me to say more, and horniness got in the way? I'll never be able to ask her now—I doubt I'll ever see her again. Maybe if the performers were Japanese, even if they said all the exact same things, the whole thing would have felt different. There was a particular atmosphere there, an informal conversation about the war that was about to begin, a conversation that could never have happened in a room full of only Japanese people. I can't even imagine it. If a group of Japanese people tried to create the same scene, it would feel wrong, like a fake plastered-on smile, and I wouldn't go anywhere near it.

The guy and me got out of the taxi and went into a convenience store for water and beer. Then we picked a hotel at random, because one was just as good as another, and got a room. It had a little fridge. That was all we needed. We were both drunk to the point of exhaustion, pretty much numb. I couldn't say for sure exactly where we got out of the taxi. I remember that the big intersection, the one in front of Shibuya Station that's always swarming with people, was as busy as usual even that late at night, so we must have gotten out around there. It would have been a little embarrassing to ask the driver to let us off by Love Hotel Hill, so we probably said that the big intersection was fine. But the driver was just a regular old guy, and we were so messed up, we probably didn't feel like walking and didn't care if he knew what we were doing, and maybe we had him drop us off by the Bunkamura. There was a Sunkus convenience store across from the 109 building, so we went there first. He wanted another beer. I didn't need any more alcohol. He bought a 500ml can. I got a litre of Evian. And also some chocolate. Whenever I get drunk and pass out, I wake up with my mouth feeling all dry and gross, like I'm about to come down with a cold. Even when I'm not that drunk, the air conditioning in love hotels is always pretty harsh, it dries you out more than anything else, which makes me feel sick, so if I don't remember to bring water I always regret it, which has happened a bunch of times, so to make sure it never happens again I think about how bad it was and always make sure to buy myself some water, no matter how drunk I am. At this point it's basically a physical reflex. The chocolate I got just because I love chocolate and thought I might want some later. I thought I would eat it when we got to the room, but that didn't happen. We had only just met, so as soon as we got to the room we undressed and had sex. I didn't get so entirely carried away that

I forgot about the chocolate, but I never got around to eating it the whole time we were there, and when we finally left the hotel I took the chocolate home with me. I ended up eating it at my place, while watching the news about the war.

After sex the first time we had sex again without stopping to rest, but he seemed fine, so I figured we might as well keep going, and then I was like this pace is kind of intense, but we kept at it, full speed. Eventually he slowed down, and then he passed out. I figured I'd get some sleep too—though it wasn't like I was feeling sad to be left awake alone or anything like that—so I slept. We both slept for the same amount of time, very fair and egalitarian, maybe two hours. But it seemed to pass in no time at all. He woke up first and started touching me, which woke me up. I started touching him back, and before long it was like okay, here we go again. I think at that point we both had every intention to keep going like that forever. It turned out not to be forever, of course, more like three or four or five times. At some point, a feeling settled on both of us that we were cutting the cord of time. You know, time which is always pushing us forwards, pushing us forwards, and even if we want it to slow down a little it never listens, so we give up hope of it ever letting up, but for now, just for now, time felt like it'd been unplugged and we had been given a reprieve. That feeling filled our bodies little by little, or maybe it came all at once, but there it was. That was what we wanted, so we tried to make it happen, and it actually did.

Like all love hotels, this one had no clock in the room, and we didn't want to know the time. Of course we both had our phones. But they were turned off and tucked away in the mesh pockets of our bags. The bags themselves we set down against the wall farthest from the bed, because we didn't want to have to see them, we didn't want them to even exist. We were trying to banish time from our little world, to make it possible for us to say, what's this time thing anyway? We'd have sex, then lie there all mellow. At some point we'd drift off into unconsciousness, beautifully, unaware who fell asleep first. After a short while one of us would wake up, then the other would wake up or be woken up. Then we'd have sex again. Since our little world had no clocks and no sun, it was hard to say for sure whether it was two days or three days or even just one.

But eventually we got hungry. We hadn't eaten since we'd checked in, and we were starved. I didn't think a love hotel was like a regular hotel where you could go out for a meal and come back, but we called the front desk and they said it was no problem. So we decided to head to Centre Street and find somewhere to eat. We put on the clothes that we had yanked off and left balled up on the floor.

Until we opened the door of the hotel we didn't know if it was day or night. Neither of us had been wondering which it was. Turned out it was daytime. We could see the sun in the narrow stretch of sky visible between the buildings that rose in front of us. The sky was murky, the same exact colour as a cloud. But to us that was the only colour the sky had ever had. The sun looked the same as it did the last time we had seen it, which made us feel a twinge of nostalgia, weird as that sounds. We walked down the hill towards the Bunkamura. We passed a barber shop and could hear the "Tamori" show on the TV inside. So it had to be lunchtime. *Where should we go? How about one of those, you know, lunch buffets all over Shibuya?* We walked up and down Centre Street, checking out the options, and settled on a place that I'd heard about, an Indian restaurant with a ¥950 all-you-can-eat buffet. It was right near the big inter-section. I had been wanting to try this place, but for someone like me with a shitty part-time job ¥950 is kind of a lot for lunch. But hey, the day was kind of an exception, and so we went on in. *This could end up being like the best curry we've ever had,* he said with a laugh. It was for sure the most curry we ever had. And even though we were both low-wage earners, we both wanted a lassi so bad that we shelled out the extra ¥250 and chugged it down.

During the days and nights I spent with him, things felt different. I wasn't in my everyday mode, I was somewhere special. I realized this when we came down the hill to the flat area by Shibuya Station, and it was like we were walking around on the bottom of a huge empty swimming pool bathed in sunlight, although I probably felt the difference earlier, back in the hotel, and even back at the performance, when the feeling first started stirring. Now we were walking in the same Shibuya as always, but it felt like I was travelling in a foreign country. Weird. Then I began to worry that if I kept thinking how weird it was, then that special mode I was in would evaporate and everything would go back to the way it is all the time. So I made up my mind not to pay any attention to this feeling. But after a bit I began to feel I didn't have to worry because the feeling didn't seem to be that fragile after all, that it wouldn't disappear so easily, and once I realized that I relaxed. I stayed in that special mode for the whole time we were together, which was a really amazing thing. I didn't think I'd ever be so lucky again. Because after that mode switched off, the next several days were terrible. But I don't think that cancels out the special feeling of those few days in that mode. I have never once wished they'd never happened.

Some tiny part of me kept asking, *how is it that I'm feeling this way, like I'm on holiday, and what does it mean?* And then I felt like I hit on a kind of answer, and I wanted to tell him about it. But we were busy eating curry, so I didn't bring it up. Once we went back to the hotel and had sex again and were in the interval before the next round, I told him.

We took a different route back to the hotel, and when we were waiting to cross the big Shibuya intersection a protest march was going by below the huge digital billboard on the Tsutaya Building. The billboard was flashing clips of the week's hit music videos, and right under the music and the dancing was a news ticker that said LIMITED CRUISE MISSILE BOMBARDMENT OF BAGHDAD BEGINS, and when we read that we were like, I guess the war really started. It was the first time I had ever seen a protest march, and just like the foreign girl at the performance said, the column of marchers, which included some foreigners, was surprisingly narrow. And the air swirling around the marchers was so calm. From close up, I could feel it.

Like the feeling on a train a little after morning rush hour. The procession went through the intersection, then angled down towards Aoyama. When the end of the march started to fade in the distance, we headed home to the hotel. Yeah, funny how at that moment going home became the reverse of normal going home. Going up Love Hotel Hill totally felt like going home. We had only stood watching the march for a tiny stretch of time, so we didn't give it too much thought, but later it kept popping back into my mind. Like we would be licking each other all over, wordlessly, almost automatically, and the image of the march would creep in to fill the space.

We walked to where there was only a slight slope, so slight you could call it level, across from Book 1st and near the Don Quijote discount store. Then the hill got steep, but it wasn't far to our hotel. By the time we were back in our room it felt like we had been gone a long while, though it couldn't have been more than two hours. It hit me that I had actually been missing the room! And the feeling grew stronger. In the next instant it filled me completely. It was the first time I had ever experienced such an instant attachment. I didn't know such a thing was even possible. That feeling's been with me ever since, much softer, but always there. Like being homesick. I wish I didn't feel that way, but I haven't been able to shake it. When it first happened I tried to ignore it. That was one of the reasons we kept having sex.

Then I noticed that he was pressing his hands against his groin, alongside his penis. At first I thought it was because pressing like that felt good to him, but then I wondered if all this sex might be starting to make him hurt. I figured it out when I saw him close his eyes, like he was willing his penis not to hurt where it was getting raw and chafed. If you're not feeling good we can stop, is what I should have said, but even if I had, he probably would have been like no, it's fine, and still kept going, I bet.

When we first got back to the hotel we started kissing, and our mouths tasted like curry and yoghurt. It made us laugh. The sex started, but the pace was much more relaxed than it had been before. Maybe we were both getting a little bored with it. The intervals we spent talking between the sex got longer and longer too. Maybe the boredom was because of having sex with the same person over and over, and maybe talking was getting easier because we had spent all this time together. Anyway, in the course of talking we decided that we would end this thing between us after two more nights. Two more nights would mean that in total we would have been at the hotel four nights. We both thought that was like the right amount of time. The limit. Pretty soon we would run out of money. But we didn't have to leave just yet. I had several ¥10,000 notes. He had almost nothing on him, though.

The sex was totally different now, the rhythm and the way we were doing it. The excitement we'd felt at the beginning was over, replaced by a sentimental feeling from knowing that the moment was going to end and a crazy kind of calculation that kept us going longer than we might have so that later we wouldn't feel like we had missed out. But even that had its limits. We took long breaks, whereas at the beginning there were hardly any breaks at all. At one point, he said, *so this is like, this is probably just me, but in a couple of days we're going to leave this hotel, right, and I feel like maybe the war'll be over by then too. Am I just being optimistic? But I mean, the difference in power is so totally obvious. And like the Gulf War was over real quick, just one pinpoint assault...* When he said this and didn't finish the sentence, we were lying side by side, staring at the stains on the ceiling. By that time we knew every little mark and discolouration, knew them by heart, which was a sign that little by little we were feeling like it was time to leave.

*

Him: *Hey, you know, this whole time we've been here we haven't turned on the TV, you know that? I mean, we've just been doing it non-stop, maybe that's why. But anyway, if we made it this long without TV, let's leave it off. What do you think?* Her: *Sure.* Him: *Yeah? Okay, great. Actually, I was going to suggest that when we got here, I just didn't. But it happened that way, it kind of just worked out. So like, we have no idea what's happening with the war now, right? That's fine, you know. When we go back to our own places, when we turn on the TV, it'll be like, hey, the war's over! That's how I'm thinking this whole scenario plays out. Like, man, the war ended almost as soon as it started, and then we'll be like, in hindsight it was all for the best. And at that point we'll be by ourselves but we'll each think the same thing. And then I'll be like, see, it happened just like I said it would, and I'll be all pleased with myself. And then you* (although he didn't really say the word "you" out loud, he kind of swallowed it) *will be like, oh, it's exactly how he said it'd be. And then we'll be like, wait a second, that means that we were doing it for the whole war. That's pretty awesome, that's what we'll think. While we were fucking our brains out, the war started and ended. Like, instead of love and peace, it'd be sex and war. I don't really know what I'm saying. But when I think about it happening that way, it kind of feels like... like we're a part of history. I was thinking like, there's a good chance I'll think back on this time right before I die.*

They had sex again. The ejaculation seemed to drain his cheekbones, but he didn't complain, didn't say anything, even though his penis felt like rubber to him. He knew he only had to hang on a little while longer. Now she did most of the talking. He listened to her, meanwhile applying pressure to his groin, trying to look casual about it. She talked about how she felt like she was on holiday, way different from her everyday mode, how Shibuya felt like a foreign country when they were out walking, and while she talked she stretched her left leg up towards the ceiling. She spoke each word as if she was finding it on the street and picking it up. And then she changed the leg she was stretching. He thought about what she was saying as he watched her stretching her legs and said, *so what would you call what we're doing now? What is this, a life? A way of life? Whatever, to be blunt, when I think about just keeping on like this, I mean think about it, it's impossible, right? We've got to face the facts. We don't have the money, for one thing. And really, how long can we keep this up, anyway?*

He kept on talking: *So, as far as money goes, I've got only like ¥2,000 yen on me. I know, sorry about that. But if we go to an ATM, I should have maybe ¥30,000 or ¥40,000 in the bank. My job pays once a month, so it's a low period for me now...* It was at this point that the two of them decided to call it. *The day after tomorrow we'll leave here and go back to our own places and by then the war'll probably be over.* When he said this, her response was, *it'll be like going home not knowing if Japan won their World Cup match today and then putting on the news to find out, you know, that kind of nervous feeling.*

Neither one of them was certain who was the first to suggest they end it on the fifth day. Maybe he said to her: *I mean I can't imagine you could've been thinking you wanted to stay here like this with me forever anyway, right? And you can say it. I mean I feel the same way, so we might as well both say it.* She said, *okay,* and he said, *okay.* They both had a feeling of release, like a fake tear duct that suddenly came unblocked. When they both said okay, by chance their voices overlapped perfectly, seamlessly, in a way that felt almost like another miracle. Their voices had matched so perfectly that they couldn't even crack a joke about it. Instead they both tried to pretend it hadn't happened. Then he started talking again, *and like, this thing between us, it's probably not going to turn into like a lifelong connection, is it? But, and this is just what I think, but it's not that a lifelong connection is somehow more special, or that we didn't make a lifelong connection because this wasn't special, or because we couldn't make that kind of connection, it's not like that at all. You get what I'm saying, right?* She said she got it. *And,* he went on, *I think that's like luck, I mean I think that spending time, days, like this with someone who understands that, that's incredible. Not everybody would understand that. I think it's super-incredible. But you could see someone saying, what's so incredible about it? All you two did was fuck the whole time.*

They needed to check what time it was. First, they had sex. It felt different from before because time was back in the picture. He pulled the phone out of his bag, which had been tossed in the corner of the room. Their moment that seemed to go on forever was coming to an end. The LCD screen showed three in the afternoon. They had guessed it was night, and only a few hours left before morning. He turned the phone off. Since they had more time than expected, they had sex some more, casually. She was worrying about the pain in his groin, but he said he was fine, so she made up her mind not to worry about it. They spent the time until the morning having sex, and resting, and every so often he reached for his phone to check the time. This was repeated through the hours, and they couldn't quite tell if it felt like the hours were moving quickly or slowly. The passing of time seemed slow, but if they took their eyes off it for an instant it seemed to skip ahead. Before long the digital numbers told them it was morning. Just a bit past eight. They lay on their backs, and he held his phone at arm's length, raised it towards the ceiling, while they brought their faces close to watch the seconds flash on the screen, to watch minutes go by. It was time to leave. They put their clothes on and gathered their things together. That didn't take any time at all. He dialled the NTT information number for date and time, brought the phone up to his ear and listened. Of course what was announced was the exact same as the display on his phone. But just seeing it on his screen, he didn't quite believe it.

When they stepped out of the room, a feeling washed over them of something coming to an end, a stronger feeling than it had been before. She paid for their stay at the desk and they went out into the day. The light stabbed at their eyes, giving them a headache like a hangover. They walked. The ATM on the way opened at 8:45, so they had timed their departure accordingly. *What bank do you use?* she asked. He answered, *Hokuriku*. She didn't know they had a branch in Shibuya. But they did, in the same building as the Lotteria. She waited on the sidewalk while he withdrew the cash. When he came out, he handed her ¥20,000. *What's with this 20,000? Your share is more than that*, she said. But that was almost all he had in his account, and he let her see the receipt that showed the ¥20,000 withdrawal and an account balance that was only in two figures. They walked to Shibuya Station. One was headed to the Toyoko Line, the other to the Yamanote Line. *Bye* was all they said, and they parted ways. But after he left, she lingered, didn't go to her train. She knew that if she got on her train and rode away from Shibuya, then she would lose this Shibuya that felt like a foreign country and her non-everyday mode would disappear and probably never come back. She wanted to keep the feeling just a bit more, so she decided to stay. But only a little while longer. She walked back the way they had just come, towards Love Hotel Hill, as if she had left something behind and was going to collect it. She worried that having already gone to the station the special feeling would have vanished, but it was still there. She turned the corner past the Bunkamura, nearly scraping the building with her shoulder, and came to the foot of the hill where their hotel was. The sloping street caught the morning light and glistened like frost. The air smelt like last night's garbage. Utility poles rose up from the sidewalk. One pole near her had a plastic trash can attached to it, and next to it was a large dog. The dog was stooped forwards snuffling, rooting around in the garbage spilling out of the trash can. But when she looked again, she saw that it wasn't a dog at all. What she'd thought was a dog's head was actually a human ass, the bare ass of a human being. It was a homeless person taking a shit. She felt the sudden urge to vomit, her throat constricting audibly. The homeless person turned towards her, still squatting. It wasn't a sharp look, more like the mild attitude someone might have listening to the wind blow. Shocked, she turned away, trying not to be too obvious, making like she too was listening to the wind, but she had in fact jerked away violently. She started walking along the side of Bunkamura, following the breeze that was blowing. After a few steps she started to run. She knew there was a toilet in Bunkamura, but the building was closed. She didn't know of any other public toilet around and the shops hadn't opened yet. There was nothing she could do. Her vomit erupted out of her and splattered onto the street. It wasn't the sight of someone shitting on the sidewalk that made her vomit, it was revulsion at herself for not knowing a human being from an animal. She realized this as the vomit was coming out of her, and even after it stopped.

She stood in place until she calmed down, then walked away from the puddle of her filth, pretending it had nothing to do with her. Some of the vomit had gotten on her clothes. She went back to the station and this time went through the wicket. While she wiped off her clothing with toilet paper in the station restroom, her special Shibuya vanished, replaced by the same old Shibuya as always.

MY PLACE IN PLURAL

THE PHONE IS NESTLED between my belly and my thighs as I lie on my side on the futon. It must look like I'm warming an egg. In my mind I keep hearing a line from a song I listen to a lot, although I'm not listening to it at the moment. I have no reason to try to block it out, so it's been playing over and over. Today is a Friday like any other. But I decided to stay home from my part-time job. I don't feel like doing anything at all.

At this point I've only made up my mind to stay home, and I haven't called in to tell them yet. The rumpled white sheet forms a ridge around my body, an almost perfect square enclosure which I'm finding it surprisingly hard to move from.

The song in my head was recommended by Naka-kido, one of my husband's friends, and my husband listened to it but it wasn't really his thing, so he didn't burn a copy or play it a second time, but I liked it, and ended up listening to it all the time.

My left hand keeps running through my hair, like I'm testing its thickness.

It's morning. The futon mattress is nearly flat and has these soy sauce stains and other discolourations. Even if I tried, I wouldn't be able to get them out.

At around two in the morning (I could pinpoint the exact time if I checked my phone but I can't be bothered), I got a text from somebody named Wakabayashi. I don't know anybody by that name, so it's probably somebody my husband knows. The text said something about the first anniversary of Nakakido's death coming up and everyone should get together. Somehow instead of the text going to my husband, or just to my husband, I was included in the text, or maybe it only came to me. I was still awake when it came in, so I read it then. It didn't make me sad, if anything it made me feel kind of uncomfortable, since I don't remember my husband telling me something had happened to Nakakido. I thought he was still alive.

My husband was at work when the text came in, cooking at a diner until I think 6:00 a.m. At the moment he's somewhere killing time until his next job starts at ten or eleven. He's probably getting some food or napping. I think about sending him a text.

But my fingers don't make a move.

The song is still on repeat in my head. My left arm is under me, pressed against the sheet. I'm not looking at the glass pane of the sliding door, but I know that the light pouring in is milky, maybe because I was looking at the door before, or maybe I can just tell without looking.

I hear the tinny melody played by the garbage truck in the distance. I have the feeling that if I get up right now and move really quickly, I could probably get the trash out in time. I've been able to before. I think about it but I know that today I won't be taking out the trash. I doubt I'll be getting out of bed.

The couple times that I managed not to miss the garbage collection, the sanitation guys were finishing loading up and about to leap onto the back of the truck when they noticed me running towards them, sandals flapping, and they were nice enough to wait for me.

My phone buzzes. I'm thinking it must be my husband.

My phone is red, and seeing it lying upside down like it is now makes me think it looks like a tiny little flipped-over sports car. This isn't the first time I've thought that.

It turns out the phone buzz was a phantom buzz. I stroke the body of the phone. How come the sun is shining outside and everyone's running around but I don't feel the least urge to do anything? How come I don't care? The light in the room feels heavy, like a chunk of ice that's starting to melt and the edges are beginning to get soft and round.

Any time my phone vibrates I get the distinct feeling that I knew it was about to happen a few seconds before it does.

I notice now that I have two unread messages which came in after the text from Wakabayashi. One is from my mother. The time stamp says exactly 4:00 a.m. I read the message and shake my head several times, trying to get my hair out of my eyes. But that doesn't do the job, so I brush them off with my hand.

A while back I accidentally left a sweater at my mother's house. Her text was asking if I was planning to come and get it. It's the third time my mother has asked. Maybe the fourth.

It's a sweater with a half-circle fringe, beige, I think, but it could be lavender. Not once has my mother offered to send it to me. At one point I told her it wasn't the season for sweaters, it was summer, but she wrote back that in summer you need a sweater because of air conditioning. It's now September of 2005, so the sweater's been there over a year.

The hum of the refrigerator feels like it's coming from a living thing, and the noise fills the room. It sits against the wall, across from the sliding glass door that's next to the futon where I'm lying. It sounds louder than usual, like the volume is turned up, forcing me to pay attention to it.

In front of the cabinet under the kitchen sink, which I can't see from where I'm lying, are two empty 500ml cans of cheap beer that my husband drank a few days ago. I placed the cans there when I was straightening up.

That song is on repeat in my mind again, having crept up on me without my noticing, and I move suddenly from thinking about the message from Wakabayashi to thinking about Nakakido, but then that floats away too, and I'm free to just listen to the song. Then I realize that the song is no longer playing, which surprises me slightly.

Now that I think about it, I've only been to my mother's once since last September. She always brews a huge pot of coffee. Any time I go to see her I end up having way more coffee than I should. For some reason, my sweater never came up. We had both forgotten about it, and I went home without it. The next day I got a text from my mother saying that I should have taken the sweater home with me.

The big toe on my right foot has found itself atop the middle toe. There's a thin film of sweat making my toes sticky, which may be why they're in that position. I move the big toe on my left foot so it's doing the same thing.

The other text is from a friend. It's a photo of a stuffed animal that she had washed and was hanging out to dry.

There's still more than an hour before I'm supposed to be at work. It's too early to call, no one's there yet. Although someone could have gone in early. My phone is already in my hand.

The hum of the refrigerator is insistent.

The weather's changing and there's a virus going around, so I decide to use that as my excuse. I cough, and then I flip open my phone. The sound it makes, *ka-chik*, even though I've heard it a million times, I still think it's a great sound. Sometimes I get in the mood to hear the sound and I pop the phone open then shut it several times. But now I just open it once.

My body makes a curve, bent at the hip like a bow. I wriggle against the futon, lift both arms over my head and stretch them back as far as they can go, like I'm trying to turn my armpits inside out.

I'm thinking that when I get a real buzz on my phone, I should pay close attention to exactly what it feels like so that I'll know to react only when there's a vibration that meets or surpasses that level of sensation, and any time the vibration doesn't meet that level of sensation I'll know that it's just a phantom buzz, and that I can ignore it. But I know that at the moment I'm not up to worrying about it.

It's when I stretch lying down like I just did that I can feel how my spine isn't straight. I spend a moment wondering whether people who keep their ringtone on for when they get a call or a text do it because they're trying to avoid being bothered by phantom buzzes like I am.

My laptop is where I left it on the nightstand, still on, still open, but the screen is dark, sleeping. I twist around to look at it, kind of rotating, ending up on my stomach. The sheet under me gets pulled along and ends up a little bunched.

The white body of my laptop is not exactly in mint condition. I've had the same computer for nearly three years. But I still haven't named it yet.

I catch sight of my nails, which are painted white. I've never once got any illustrations or decorations done on my nails. They're just all white.

Before my laptop went to sleep, it got pretty hot

but now it's cooled off. I strike a key and the screen wakes up. I was up late reading blogs, dozing off and waking up to read some more, and now the last one I was reading gradually returns to the wakening screen. When that happens, the flecks of dust that were visible on the dark surface of the screen vanish.

The page I have open is the blog cache of someone with the username "armyofme", who according to the profile is a twenty-eight-year-old woman (that makes her two years younger than me) who "works as a call centre operator at a company that provides outsourced help-desk services, currently dealing with enquiries for an internet service provider in the process of transitioning to fibre-optic cables", and she blogs about all the callers with their claims that annoy her day after day, and about all her co-workers who are just as bad as the callers, stringing her words together like a stream of curses. armyofme writes a new blog post almost every day.

I just stumbled upon her blog today, I mean last night. How I found it is because there was this guy in my class at art school who used to do comedy stuff, and somebody told me he and another guy have an act that's been getting them on TV, but since I don't watch much TV I never knew about it, so I started searching a bunch of things related to my friends from back in school, trying different combinations of words, and after maybe three hours I found myself on armyofme's blog.

I can hear the garbage truck coming around again. I now realize that when the song on repeat in my head switched off earlier it was because of the garbage truck music.

armyofme had an entry from a few months ago where she wrote about how watching the guy from my art class perform on TV was encouraging for her, but then she got used to seeing him all the time and she stopped feeling encouraged and thought about how he must be having fun, but also that maybe it looks like fun but it's probably hard work, and in any case he has to be making good money so she doesn't feel bad about being a little jealous.

It's pretty normal for me to go looking for websites or blogs or whatever that are about people I know and to end up spending hours surfing. I always feel sleepy, it's been so long since I've felt fully clear-headed and awake that I've basically forgotten what that's like, so for years my whole waking life has been powering down, and now that's just my body's default mode. But when I look for blogs and I find a good one and my eyes are glued to the screen, some substance starts flowing from the LCD and pumping into me, and my sleep threshold shoots up, like blood sugar when you're munching on sweets, so no matter how tired I feel I can still stay awake.

I stretch my body so that I can feel the crook in my spine. I think about people I know who are armyofme's age and who might write something like this, and I picture the faces of a few girls who could be armyofme. But I can't say which of them it could be. I mean, I can't even remember their names.

Last night, or this morning, reading armyofme's blog kept me energized until I hit my sleep threshold. Even when I did pass that point, I would only nod off for the shortest while and then wake up and get right back to it. I was reading another blog too, before armyofme's, not anybody who I'm connected to in any way, it's a guy who writes letters to his college friend who died in an accident the year before. I came across it when I was searching for things about Nakakido.

Not that that blog had anything to do with Nakakido. It must have been one of the other search terms beside his name that landed on it. I ended up reading some of it, but only a little. The writing was a mess, like it was written by someone in a confused mental state. In fact I started to think that there was no such person as the dead friend, and I gave up on it.

In armyofme's newest post, or anyway the one with the most views, she wrote how *people on the phone say talking to an operator like you* (meaning her) *isn't getting me* (them) *anywhere, let me talk to your manager. It happened today, but people who say stuff like that have no idea the way the system works, they probably think that if they keep screaming to talk to somebody more important they'll eventually get to whoever's in charge and can finally give whoever it is a piece of their mind and get some satisfaction, but that's more or less impossible, like no matter how hard they try they'll never reach anyone with any authority at the fibre-optic cable company because the system is specifically designed to keep that from ever happening, so maybe if their issue is really serious and could turn into a high-profile lawsuit and get picked up by the media and turn into a big story they might get somewhere, but short of that their call will just come into our outsourced call centre, and the highest up it could go would be to the project leader in charge of the fibre-optic cable company account, but even that's extremely unlikely, because we lowly operators know very well that if we gave in every time someone demanded to talk to our manager things would get messy for us, and we've been told to absolutely refuse those kinds of demands, so unless there's a pushover girl who gets nervous and does what the caller wants, it'll never happen. And anyway our call centre is*

*just doing work that the fibre-optic cable company has
outsourced, the fibre-optic cable company is my company's
client, and I'm sure they've told us to deal with whatever
claims that come in (I don't actually know that, since I'm
not on the business side of things, I'm just guessing, but
I'd bet I'm right), since we're not located anywhere near
them, we're in Ikebukuro, way past the park to the west
of the station in a nine-storey building in an area that's
gone out of style, on the sixth through ninth floors, and I
sit on the eighth floor (actually I don't even know where
the client is, though they must be somewhere in Tokyo).
Anyway, that's how it is, so when people call about their
claim I tell them the person you're complaining to isn't the
person you want to be complaining to, and they say they
know that which is why they're shouting that they want
to talk to my manager, and the people who are shouting
are the ones I want to tell that no matter how much they
kick and scream they'll never get to the person they're
looking for. Of course I can't actually say that...* That's
the kind of stuff in armyofme's blog. In other entries
she actually laid out the details of the clients' claims,
going on and on. I fell asleep after a little while, but
before I did, when I was awake, I read all of it. Every
so often I would accidentally click on one of the ads
flashing in the sidebar, for a new DVD release or a
soft drink, or an online credit card application or

a job site, and every time I did that a new browser window would open up, and in the few seconds while the page loaded, I felt like I was holding out hope for something, though I'm not sure what. But as soon as the content came on screen my hope vanished. I would go back to the blog and keep reading.

My toes are facing downwards, pressed against the sheet. They're painted white, same as my fingernails. I work the rumpled bunches in the sheet between my toes so that they're touching the sensitive skin in there that's not used to being touched. But I can't tell from the feel of that skin between the toes whether the sheet is dry or damp, damp from my sweat or maybe from the humidity in the room.

I think about my husband, between his job at the all-night diner and the next one, and I get the urge to send him a text and tell him to hang in there. But the best I can manage is the most basic message, something like *hope you're doing okay* and a couple other trite words that mean basically nothing.

I let out a huge yawn.

There's a spiderweb on the ceiling, but it's only in the early stages, just a few threads stretched out, not yet intersecting.

Whenever I get a feeling like I just had, like I want to express my appreciation for someone, as soon as I start trying to write them a text I start to focus instead on how exhausted my body feels and how that's all I can pay attention to, and by that point I couldn't care less about any nice feelings I had.

My body lies there, and I can't seem to get any energy into it. I almost feel like I might never find any energy ever again. I send the text to my husband, though it's just a very short one. The digital signal flies off through a cloudy sky. But the sun is burning hot behind the clouds, so it doesn't even really feel like a cloudy day, more like a blue sky that's turned white. My husband will be working at the drugstore today, a job he just started, and I actually do hope it goes all right for him. The display on my phone says *9 September*, which means it's been nine days since he started there. I'm still staring at the ceiling. I don't see the spider anywhere.

More than once I've wondered if my husband has a blog or something like that, and I've tried all kinds of search terms, but I haven't found anything.

The way the panels on the ceiling are joined together, the pattern of artificial wood knots, the circle markings that look like scars where the panels are fitted to the joists, they all look like elements in a diagram or a floor plan, only instead of looking up at it I feel like I'm peering down at it from above. I somehow slip right into seeing it that way, and almost immediately the illusion spreads to all my senses. My body has been secreting oils all night, from my face especially. I run three fingertips from the top of my nose to below my chin and back up again, and even though it feels like a chore I keep tracing the same path back and forth.

By now my husband is sitting on the second floor of Becker's café in the JR Iidabashi Station, in the non-smoking area, the seat against the wall at the far end of the counter. He's finished his coffee and is slumped forwards, napping until it's time for his next job. The text I send him makes his phone vibrate briefly, but he's not awake, so he doesn't catch it in real time.

His phone is on a dull white plastic tray covered in scratches and dings. When the text comes in, there are two sounds, the phone's own buzz and the slight rattling between the phone and the tray.

Across the room from the counter, against the opposite wall, there's a four-top where five high-school boys in uniform are sitting. One of them is on a chair he brought over from another table, and one of them keeps saying, Let's open it guys, come on, let's open it. I don't know what he's talking about.

I turn my body so I'm once again looking upward, more or less. I bend my right knee, then try to place the outside ankle against the left side of the hollow behind my left knee.

When I read armyofme's blog, I didn't have any intention of committing any of it to memory, but now the idea of what she wrote, the general feeling, and also some specific turns of phrase, they're whirling around inside my head just like the melody I wasn't trying to memorize, and they're blooming and morphing as they spin. I don't resist it, I just let it happen.

By now the melody is gone.

My laptop hasn't been touched for several minutes and now it's gone back to sleep. The screen faded out, taking with it armyofme's account of her worst caller of the day. As soon as she heard the caller's voice she knew this one wasn't going to be easy, and when she asked for the customer number the caller rattled off the eight digits, not clumsily like reading it off a piece of paper but fast like from the practise of having been asked for it so many times, so that she knew for sure this caller's called before, and in fact when she entered the customer number into the system she saw that the first claim was a month ago but the caller's service still hadn't been restored, which she knew had to be aggravating in the extreme, and when she checked the notes, there were a whole bunch that other service operators had entered, and she saw that the caller had tried to get help more than ten times and had complained to the operators that the only explanation for the terrible service was that they were purposely trying to stonewall him, and one of the notes was from an operator who got this caller three times and wrote an exasperated line in the call log about losing at Russian roulette. The blog went on and on, past the bottom of the page, waiting for me to scroll down, but it's all vanished now. I can see dust against the black screen again. At the moment I don't feel like wiping it off.

Near my laptop is a fashion magazine I was reading before bed, nearly all in full colour, thick and heavy because of the large number of ads, splayed open on the floor. The vinyl flooring has a wood panel design.

My husband is wearing a blue T-shirt. It has an illustration of a washing machine on it. But he's slumped over at the counter, so no one can see it.

When we looked at this place before moving in, the tatami was old and discoloured, so the day after we moved in we bought a roll of the vinyl flooring at a department store in Kichijoji, which is a straight shot to here, so even though it was heavy and tough to manoeuvre, we got it home on the train and laid it down over the tatami. At the time we were real pleased with our choice, with the wood pattern, with the whole idea of covering the tatami with the flooring. But we don't feel that way any more.

The day we laid down the flooring, my husband was wearing the same blue T-shirt. He was down on all fours, and I was standing behind him looking at him, and I remember my eyes fixing on the blue of his shirt.

Once a page from a magazine or a newspaper sticks to the flooring, it's stuck. It's impossible to peel it away cleanly, and it always leaves a splotchy pattern of the pulpy soft part of the paper, looking like the connected waterways on an atlas page of a marshy part of the world. The splotches of paper get walked on and rubbed by the bottoms of our feet until they turn dark grey.

When it's raining and the humidity is high enough, the flooring gets slick.

Sometimes I want to read lying on my back, holding my magazine over me, and sometimes I want to lie on my stomach and read. But a magazine this heavy I can't read on my back. The pages printed in colour smell of ink. I read on my stomach for a while, propped on my elbows to hold up the weight of my shoulders, but before long parts of me start to ache and I can't hold that pose very long either.

I lie on my back. I stare at the ceiling and stretch my whole body out, my trunk and legs pulling in opposite directions, like I was trying to rip myself in half at the waist. The ceiling doesn't stretch, or contract, it just looks the same as always.

At the counter where my husband is sleeping, on the tray he has pushed to one side, next to his mobile phone, is a white mug. There's a centimetre or so of coffee left in it, which looks more like a shadow at the bottom. Beside the mug is a small wicker basket with the crumpled wrapper that held the hamburger my husband ate before he fell asleep.

One corner of this wrapper has managed to escape being crumpled, it's kind of flat, and on the back side of it is a splatter of ketchup. In the centre of the tray are a handful of napkins my husband grabbed from the dispenser but didn't end up using, still in the same bunch from when he pulled them out.

Before he dozed off he pushed the tray to his right so he could put his head down on the counter in front of him. One hand lies on top of the other wrist, and his forehead lies on top of his two hands. He doesn't need to get going yet, and he's been in that position for a while. It won't be long before his hands start to go numb.

His hands smell like sanitizer. The smell mixes with the smell of the meat he pulls from tightly packed plastic bags in the freezer, that meat patty smell, and the smell of the sweet sauce that goes on the meat. His hands smell of all that, as does his hair.

I no longer have the urge to stroke my hair, and instead I run the palm of my hand over my cheek, to my chin bone, to the curve of where my jaw meets my neck. I apply pressure to my chin, so that it hurts a little, so that I can really feel the bone in there.

My husband's bag, stuffed to bursting, rests under his legs, crammed between his stool and the counter. His hair looks greasy.

Sometimes when my husband is sleeping I sneak my face close to his hands, so that I can smell them. It's not that I like the smell of meat. I actually find it disgusting. But I keep doing it because I want to make sure I still find it disgusting.

As for his hair, as soon as he shampoos, the smell goes away.

There's one TV show that I absolutely have to watch, it's on once a week, on Tuesdays at eleven, and last week when I was watching it my husband was at home. I don't know if it was because he was asleep or because he just wouldn't watch it with me but suddenly my frustration at him boiled over, and I knew I shouldn't have but I started in on him, attacking him, while my show was still on, through the end of the show, past midnight, on and on until who knows how late, basically telling him he was a good-for-nothing coward, which would have been too cruel to actually say so I didn't, but that about sums up what I was feeling.

When I was watching TV, I was lying there motionless, my body feeling heavy and tired like it is now, training my eyes on the screen, absorbing the flickering light. I can't remember what set me off, but I started saying wouldn't it be nice if we had a little more money, don't you think we should try to do something about that, I really think we should be thinking more about the future, that kind of stuff, trying to make it seem like it was just occurring to me, when of course I had it on my mind, and I was talking with an edge, and once I got going I sat up and leant forwards over my knees on the vinyl flooring.

Before long I was shouting at the top of my lungs, not holding back at all, lashing out at my husband and it was like I couldn't stop. At one point my eyes were swollen and burning. I had the vague feeling that if I really wanted to talk about this with him, it might have been better if I wasn't screaming and crying.

Thinking back to that whole thing, I start to feel the laziness in my body tighten up at the back of my neck. It could be that the tension was already there and building up and I only noticed it just then. When I was freaking out at him, I knew that we were both working, and that we weren't broke or anything, and that this tantrum I was throwing wasn't doing me or him or us any good. It's not that I understand all of that only now that I've calmed down, I was totally aware of it when I was yelling at him.

For his part, my husband didn't act hurt or angry at what I was saying, he just sat there passively taking it all in. To me, this was humiliating. Why didn't he shout back, challenge the outrageous stuff I was saying, why didn't he get mad at me? That's why I've spent so much time searching for a blog or something of his, because if he had a reason not to shout back I bet he would have written about it. But it could be that he doesn't write a blog, or that if he does it's set to private and you have to sign up or register or something to read it, or it's on a secret page on Mixi or some other social networking site that I won't be able to find. And if he did that, then I really *really* wonder what he wrote.

I make my biggest move of the day so far: I put my head where my feet were and my feet where my head was. The sheet where my head was feels damp and humid, and I'm sure that there are some parts of the sheet where my feet were that are cool and dry. I tuck my trunk towards my legs so that my body is in a wedge, then pull my legs away so I'm straight again, and repeating this four or five times rotates me around the bed like the hands rounding a clock. I was right, the sheet at the bottom is refreshingly cool.

While I was yelling at my husband, and after I was done too, he sat there scratching his left bicep like he had a stubborn itch. From his perspective my tantrum must have come out of nowhere. But for me it was a long time coming, it had been simmering, getting hotter, so that once it got to boiling there was no stopping it.

I let my head drop forwards as far as the bones in my neck will allow. Then I lean it all the way back. But I can't go so far back on my own. To get it back all the way, so that it's flush against my spine, *snap,* I'd need someone to help.

The sliding glass door beside me gives off an energy that I think is somehow like a lover who wants me, who wants to get on top of me. It's almost too much to bear.

This apartment of ours is in the one sunken spot on a swell of land, squeezed into a cluster of buildings, none of them more than five storeys, which isn't short but feels short, and somehow oppressive. There's a mix of places: apartment buildings like ours, an exam-prep school, also an Asian goods gift shop, I'm guessing, based on the fact that the window is full of origami and kanji placards on imitation Japanese paper and clothes with fabric that looks rough to the touch hanging from the curtain rods. There are a few, very few, single-family houses, and also a building with gallery space for rent a half-flight of stairs down from ground level. Our apartment building is jammed in right in the middle of all this, kind of like a child being crowded and pushed around by bigger kids. We used to say that being stuck in the middle is why our walls and floors are always sweating. But really it's because we're in the cheapest unit in the building, down on the first floor with the worst light. In winter our place feels like a swamp. It smells like one too.

I always place my futon next to the sliding glass door. Rings of grime spatter across the pane, white outlines of where the drops of condensation have dried, almost regular enough to make a pattern. Just beyond our tiny concrete balcony is a patch of land overgrown with weeds that give off a powerful grassy odour. Between the balcony railing and the wall of the next building is less than a metre.

I can't shake the idea that my husband could have a diary or a blog, whether or not I would ever be able to read it, but supposing he has one, does he write about me? When I ask myself this question, I don't know if I want the answer to be yes or no.

He's slumped over on the counter sleeping, head resting on his hands, the tips of his fingers peeking out, and they've got a faint red tint to them, like maybe he was handling a red ink-pad.

Suddenly I have the memory of staring through the glass of the sliding door and seeing two cats on the balcony, perfectly still, until they sprang up onto the rail and leapt to the next building and scrambled up the wall and out of my sight. Thinking about such a mundane scene feels a little like a premonition of death.

I notice that the two empty cans of beer I set down on the kitchen floor have tipped over.

There's mould in the bathroom, but it's also in the corners of the kitchen, and on one spot of the tatami under the vinyl flooring. I can't get it out, although I've tried. But the mould is worst in the closet, which I keep closed because the smell is really strong. We've lived here for several months now, and little by little I've got used to the mould smell and the general stickiness, so that it doesn't even really bother me any more. I'm actually a little surprised that I was able to get used to it, but I haven't told my husband. He always leaves the closet door open, which I hate.

Why do we have to live in such a nasty, musty place, it's tiny and it has no light and it reeks of mould, are we going to spend the rest of our lives here? I once said that to my husband. He said, *okay, you want to move? Okay, let's move, is that what you want?*

I didn't say anything. Instead I scooted towards him, I was sitting on the floor facing him and I unfolded my legs from under me and thrust them at him and hopped on my butt in his direction and with my outstretched legs I kicked at him over and over again. For a second he laughed, maybe thinking I was doing a special move of a hero in a kids' show, and he used his left arm to shield himself, but the next moment he whipped his arm back towards me to pin down my legs. Just before he got me I landed one good kick on his arm, right in the spot where he has three large birthmarks, which make me think of Orion's belt. But then he had me, and I couldn't move. I struggled for a bit while he held me down, but he's a man, and I doubt he even had to try very hard.

His arm on the counter at Becker's looks bulging, but it's not from muscles, it's from the bend in his elbow and from the weight of his head. There's a burn on his skin from his job in the kitchen, something must have got on him, but it's already crusting over with a scab.

After I was kicking him, as he was holding me down, I'm pretty sure this happened, I smelt something weird, and it could even have been coming from my own body, I had no idea what it was but it smelt rotten, like maybe it was the contents of a stomach, vomit about to come up. I'm thinking about it now, after it happened, and I can't believe a smell that foul could be mine. Maybe I was imagining it, because when you actually smell bad, you only pick up the littlest bit of your smell, like a whiff from somewhere far away, so maybe I wasn't really smelling it at all. But obviously I couldn't ask my husband, so I have no way of knowing for sure. If I did imagine it, then why? I mean, why did I imagine a stench like that? At the time I think I was sobbing, tears and mucus running down my face.

Slumped over on the counter, asleep, my husband's bony spine and shoulders twitch from time to time. When the spasm is big enough the counter creaks. But it's still only a tiny movement, and the noise barely registers. His back is rounded and tight at the same time. He isn't capable of letting go of all that tension, not even in his sleep.

Whenever I freak out, like I did that time, my husband always comes up with the best-sounding, most optimistic, most unrealistic solution possible.

I knew he would do it that time too, I was actually expecting it.

He loosened his hold on me. Even though he let me go I knew that I shouldn't start thrashing around again, so I stayed still. But I made sure to keep chewing him out, I said *what the hell are you talking about, moving, how could we possibly do that, and you know, we haven't even been here half a year, we can't just go from place to place, it'll cost so much fucking money, did you even stop to think about that?*

He sat there listening to me, wiping his glasses with a lens cloth which he keeps in the pocket of his favourite jeans, the ones he's always wearing. I don't think that little lens cloth had been washed in months, but he did manage to get some of the smudges off the lenses. I guess even though he doesn't wash the lens cloth itself, at least it is in his pocket when he washes the jeans, which happens once in a while. His lens cloth is here now. His jeans are inside out, stuffed into the washing machine, which I can't see from where I am. The top of the jeans is spilling out over the top of the machine.

I stretch again. First out, then up, my palms spread to the ceiling.

My husband is wearing his other jeans, the old ones, with the hole in the knee. The crotch is worn thin, with little openings where you can see the flesh of his upper thigh. His blue T-shirt is also pretty worn out. The crew-neck collar is all stretched and shapeless, and the blue is faded. It used to be bright blue. His legs follow the line of the stool towards the floor, but his feet don't touch the ground.

He listened until I stopped yelling, then waited until he was done wiping his glasses, then said to me *you're right, but you know, take the mould for instance, we knew the place was mouldy but we decided we would deal with it because our priority was cheap rent, but now that we actually live here if you can't stand the smell of the mould, then of course it's a shame to lose the money it would take to move but wouldn't moving be the best thing?* That's what he said. But why couldn't he say something like let's just stick it out for another half-year?

I grabbed a kitchen knife and hacked down on the controller cord for his game system. I'm not sure if this was before I tried to kick him and he pinned me, or after.

I severed the cord neatly. This surprised me, because I thought maybe some of the wires inside the rubber casing would put up a fight. Cutting through the cord so easily was kind of anticlimactic. But at that moment there was no room in my body, my face, my heart, to express that let-down.

My head always feels like it's full of dust balls, grey and jagged, mixed with shreds of metal, stabbing at me. I want to get rid of them, dump them out, like emptying the vacuum cleaner, but even if I managed to do that, to shake them all out, somehow I know they would appear again and multiply and fill me right back up.

If I was really so repulsed by the mould and humidity, there's no way I would be lying around here like this now. I'd get myself up and get out of these sweatpants, which have this stretched-out elastic at the waist so that I need to tie the drawstrings or the pants fall down, I'd take them off and put on some real clothes and go outside.

The alley that leads from our apartment building to the street feels like an accidental gap between the buildings, so narrow you'd have a hard time walking your bike through. There's one part of the alley that's concrete because it's part of the foundation, but most parts of the alley aren't so when it rains the ground turns to mud and shoes get all muddy. But it's been sunny the past few days, so the dirt in the alley should be dry and hard.

The street it leads to isn't much of a street either, only a car-and-a-half wide. It's closed to oversized vehicles, but they didn't make it one-way or anything, except for a stretch in the morning when it's rush hour.

I lift my right leg and point my toes, ballet-like, making one straight line. Or I guess I should say that's what I was trying to do. I can feel the tendons on the outside of my ankle straining.

The narrow street eventually turns into a wider road that's a slope with two lanes, where the sky isn't all chopped up by the buildings and you need to use the traffic mirrors because of the curves as you go down the hill. The slope levels off by the station. But you can't see the station, because there's a big bookstore in the way, you can only see it once you cross the intersection. The two-lane road goes past the station and continues on for a bit until it joins Sotobori Avenue which keeps going all the way around the moat of the Imperial Palace. There's a big sign over the avenue there, with fat white arrows on a green background that direct you to the on-ramp for the expressway.

I have the whole day to myself, but no way I'm going to work up the energy to go anywhere. If I did go anywhere, it would probably be the convenience store or somewhere for a coffee, and it'd cost money.

There is a bunch of convenience stores around the station.

I've been staring at the ceiling, and the beam running across the middle starts looking like the centre line of a soccer field.

I'd better put in that call to work.

Sometimes when I look at the sign for FamilyMart, with the blue and green stripes, the green part looks beautiful to me (just the green, not the blue). It's only at a certain time, when the light in the sky is right. Like how I feel about the red of a traffic light when dusk is about to fall and the sky is a little purple. Only thing is I don't remember at what time of day the light in the sky is right for the green in the FamilyMart sign, except that I'm sure it's not the beginning of dusk.

The area around my left bicep starts to itch, so I slide my right hand under the sheets and scratch at it through the fabric.

My husband's arm emerges from the short sleeve of his blue T-shirt, bending at the elbow in a sprawl on top of the white tray on the counter. The elbow has a birthmark, and it comes to a sharp point and looks more grimy to me than the average elbow.

When I yelled at my husband, demanding to know how he could stand to live in such a mouldy-smelling place, it wasn't because I'm physically unable to stand it, it's more the fact we have to live somewhere that's mouldy, but I don't think he understood where I was coming from. He's probably still thinking that I'm suffering from the mould smell itself, and if he's written about it in his blog, even if he didn't use any names or write enough specifics for someone to figure out who it was about, I think, speaking as someone who was there, I would be able to identify myself from the details, and if he has written about the whole mould-driving-me-crazy business, I'm sure it paints me in a terrible light.

This scenario of mine is now pretty much running on autopilot in my brain. Like maybe he ducked into an internet café for thirty minutes before work last night and wrote it, so that I could find it and read it within a few hours of him writing it. He hadn't written yesterday or the day before, so he was really feeling like he had to do it, get it written down. Like about me chopping through his controller cord with a knife, and me knowing that I could fly off the handle and destroy his controller and he wouldn't do anything to me, and even though I knew he loved his video games, I would do it anyway, and how he would say I'm a spoilt brat, only a child would act that way, and how he was surprised by my chopping through his controller cord, but his surprise was quickly taken over by anger, but he didn't blow up, he just stayed calm, he was trying to vibe me to snap out of it, and then he had this sudden impulse and he slugged me. At least that's what he would have written, even though in real life he's never hit me even once. He didn't even make a sound when I chopped the controller cord, not a peep of surprise or anger, which actually I think made more of an impact on me, but in his blog I bet he wrote that he shouted, really went off, like hey what the hell are you doing, you're acting fucking crazy!

I call work. There are people there who are all right, and people there who aren't and I don't like. One of the ones I don't like answers. But that just makes it easier for me to fake it, to recite the excuse I planned, to keep up the act for the few seconds it takes without any wavering, not feeling any remorse. I do feel a little guilty as far as my husband is concerned, though.

I mean, I'm supposed to be at work today. I just made up my mind not to go, so even if I tried to force my body to get up and go, at this point it's impossible. I've been lying on my stomach for so long it feels like I'm just another fold of the moisture that's collecting in layers all the way up to the ceiling.

I wonder what screen name my husband uses.

Once in a while my laptop whirrs and rattles, the sound of the battery vibrating as the computer performs some function or other, and I hear it every time it goes, which stirs a vague feeling of me being somewhere way deep down, like maybe at the bottom of the ocean.

I press my chin down into the futon. My sight line is just above the keyboard, and when I lower my head a little more the keys become a flat field, the LCD screen looming over the horizon. But almost immediately, seeing things like this feels weird, and all I want is to feel normal, so I flip over onto my back and look at the ceiling again. This time my eyes settle on the fluorescent light that's hanging from the ceiling. Sure enough, the circular bulbs are gargantuan. Somehow the clock on the wall is the only thing that keeps its original proportion.

If I push any key it'll wake the screen from its dark sleep, her blog still there in my laptop's cache, all the words armyofme spun out about the customers who won't give up, and all their complaints, giant text suddenly replacing the black of the night, scrolling now by themselves, on and on:

You must think I'm a real pain in the ass (in fact I do, sir), but I'm not giving up. My service has been out for a month. A month! I can't get online, I can't play my games, I feel like I'm stuck on a desert island. Is it standard practice in your industry to make all these promises in your ads that you never keep? Can you explain that to me? (No, I can't, sir.) I mean, take this phone call, all these phone calls, you don't have a toll-free number, I'm the one paying for the call, every second that ticks by, I'm paying for it, don't you think it's wrong that you make the customer pay for these calls? (Well, maybe you should hang up.) What's your name, anyway? Hello, your name? (I didn't know what else to say, so I actually told him my name.) So what do you think about all this, I mean your honest opinion, I'd really like to know, I feel like if you told me I'd be at least a little less aggravated, so will you just tell me, please? It can just be between us, I just want to know what you really think about this, so just for a second would you put aside your professional responsibilities and share with me your unfiltered, personal take on this, as a human being, I'd love to know. Will you tell me? Are the things I'm saying, in my frustration, am I missing the mark? Am I wrong about this?... He kept going and going. Having someone pour their heart out to me for so long starts to trip me up emotionally, so despite myself I agreed with him, No sir, you're not wrong, *and as soon as I said it I regretted it, but it was too late. He was silent for a moment, and then he said,* Right, that's what I thought, I'm not wrong, am I, *and it was clear that he was feeling a little better about himself, but I was thinking about the fact that my manager and my group leader were monitoring the conversation. Their computers have admin software that lets them check in at a glance* on what's happening with all the calls in the call centre. When anyone is on with the same caller for more than twenty minutes, the system automatically flags them and one of the group leaders starts listening in.

I was on the line with the caller for almost an hour until he finally ran out of energy and gave up. While I was logging the call, I got an internal page from one of the group leaders, Mr S. As expected, he gave me a soft-pedalled warning about the call: Hey there, that was a long call you had to deal with, thanks for hanging in there, good stuff... But you know, sorry, there's just one thing I wanted to touch on regarding how you handled it, if that's okay... I'm guessing you know what it is I'm going to say, so I hope you won't mind, I'm going to just jump in...

The moment I got off the line with him I was overcome by helplessness, a feeling like something was squeezing my insides. I could barely breathe. Somehow I made it to the end of the workday. I took off my headset and immediately put on my own headphones, then walked across the floor and out, first to leave. When I got on the Yurakucho Line, I still had that feeling like my innards were being crushed. I wanted to eat a whole pile of fried chicken drowned in tartar sauce. Not because I was hungry, but because I wanted to stuff myself until I felt even worse.

I ducked into the 7-Eleven near my place. There was no fried chicken with tartar sauce in the rows of bento, so

I headed to the FamilyMart a few blocks away. They had what I was looking for. The cashier warmed it up for me. I got home and went straight to my computer, where I sat consuming my chicken while I wrote in my blog all the obnoxious things the group leader said to me. I worked the strangling feeling inside me into words. As I wrote, I recalled the sound of Mr S's voice, the way my arm was fidgeting while I listened: So going forwards, let's remember, you're on our side, not the customer's side, you feel sympathetic, I get it, but we have to present a united front, so if you could remember that going forwards, that'd be great...

But even writing out what S said in as much detail as I could bear to and then uploading it didn't alleviate the squeeze on my guts one bit. If anything it made me feel worse, like my body was on the verge of spasms, and I was getting more and more frantic.

And that's when the scroll bar finally reaches the bottom and goes no farther. Then, without warning, the screen switches to a totally new layout, bringing me to a whole different blog. I see the name of the author, but I can't quite bring myself to process it, which is to say, I can't write it here. But I know right away that it's my husband's blog.

As usual, I don't know what to do with my body.

From what I read in his blog, it seems that the foul odour I worried I gave off that time but wasn't sure was real was real after all. My husband found the stench so shocking that at first he didn't even make the connection—he smelt it, but he didn't really acknowledge it, not immediately anyway, until he finally started to get where it was coming from, which was when he looked straight at me, but being unsure whether to yell at me or be worried for me, he just sat there and said nothing.

He was completely dumbstruck. He wrote, *what is she, part skunk?*

Of course he's never smelt a real skunk. But once when he was a boy he took his dog to the vet for an injection, and it wasn't the first time the dog had gotten an injection, so it knew something painful was about to happen, and as it stood there on the vet's exam table, it let out this truly noxious gas, which the vet said was the same type of reaction a skunk has, so you could say my husband has at least smelt something skunk-like before. The odour I was giving off must have been the same kind of thing, he wrote.

The larger of the two circular fluorescent bulbs in the light hanging from the ceiling is dead. It's been dead for more than a week but we haven't replaced it.

I'm bored with lying around here on my futon, I've been bored for a while now. But I know that when my husband takes the train home tonight, one of the last trains if not the last, my body will still be sprawled out on the mattress. I might even be asleep, deaf to the sound of him coming in. I can always sleep, and when I'm asleep I can sleep on and on.

But if I am awake, I might come right out and tell him that I blew off work and stayed in bed all day. Definitely not because I'm holding myself to a high standard of righteous honesty, and I would probably come right out and say it to anyone, it wouldn't have to be my husband, although he's the only person I've got, but I would say it because I want to put him in a bad mood. I have a deep need for someone to let me hurt them, I want to pull my husband down here to my level, where I'm wallowing, to be with me and to stay with me, to feel exactly what I'm feeling, I want to take these chunks of negative shit that I'm carrying around like rock candy crammed into my head and body, like bad junk that needs to be thrown away, and I want to pass them on to him, even though I'm not sure they can be passed on, I want to give him as much as I can, even a tiny bit would be enough.

But if I come right out and say to him I didn't do a worthwhile thing all day, I can't picture him giving me the reaction that I want, like making a face that shows how fed up he is. I'd be happy if he made any face at all, whether or not I could tell what it meant.

I need a reaction from him more than anything else, but he doesn't seem to grasp that. Why can't he give any of himself to me?

The bottom of my ribcage is having a shoving match with the floor, the impact only slightly absorbed by the futon and the meat around my bones.

My husband thinks that it's a good thing to be indulgent with me, he thinks that it's a way to be kind, and he's completely blind to the fact that all it does is make me feel worse about what a narrow-minded, petty, lazy bitch I am. I don't need him to be kind to me or tolerant of how I behave. He's never picked up on the fact that this is a change he needs to make. I've tried to make that clear to him again and again. But he always seems to think that his way is right, he's never tried to change, never tried to see it from my perspective, not in the least. Every so often it gets to where I can't stand it.

My husband is not the sort of person who brings work home with him, he doesn't talk about how tired he is, or complain about his co-workers. Instead he brings home beer. He likes these tall cans of cheap low-malt beer, which is what he was drinking when I chopped his game controller cord in half. Why doesn't he ever feel any rage towards me, even a little? Even when I do something like that?

When I finally calmed down, he quietly slipped out of the apartment. He was so quiet and downcast he seemed almost apologetic, not angry at all. He put on his shoes with such care that it didn't make a sound. Then he left, headed out to the closest convenience store.

It's down the hill, not all the way down, a little before the street hits the wider road.

If you go up the hill instead, there are no shops or stores. Just a postbox a few steps up. It's a gentle slope at first, with the path stretching up in a straight line. Then you come to a little tunnel. Right on the other side it gets really steep and the path starts to snake back and forth. Eventually you come to a set of stairs.

The surface of the path is asphalt, but the stairs are concrete, a concrete so white that in bright light the dirt on it shows. The asphalt smells like asphalt, and the concrete smells like concrete.

The stairs don't go all the way to the top of the hill, they stop short around twenty metres from the top. From there it's a path again. But still concrete. Regularly spaced on the concrete path are circular depressions twenty centimetres across, designed I guess to keep you from slipping.

When the slope rounds off and you can walk easily again, there's really nothing up there—a pay parking lot, a vacant lot where maybe they'll put in another pay parking lot, another site that's just dry, bare earth, a storage shed by an abandoned croquet court. There's an elementary school and a junior high school. But neither of those has anything to do with us. It doesn't make one bit of difference to us whether the school-yard's full of kids or their ghosts.

There's a library and a low-slung building that serves as the local community centre.

Part of the hilltop is a park. In the middle is a tall stand of broad-leafed trees. When you go in, though, it doesn't feel like the trees are pressing in around you. There are other trees dotting the rest of the park too. There's a long slide that dips down the side of the hill.

I sat waiting for my husband. The TV was on but I just listened, didn't watch, looked instead at my phone, reading my horoscope. As my husband approached the convenience store, he seemed to be basking in a warm light, the way it was coming from the store. Stepping inside, he took a free help-wanted weekly from the rack by the entrance.

By the time he came back home, I had finished reading my horoscope and was about to check what kind of luck he was going to have this week.

The job listings said that there was a drugstore hiring not far from our place.

The next morning my husband called exactly when the listing said they'd start taking calls. He hadn't finished his toast yet, but they were taking calls so he called. I sat there and listened while he arranged a time to go there and apply. Then the morning after that he left home and went straight to the drugstore. Before the day was over he texted me that he got the job.

He started the next day. At first it was all training. Instead of this happening at the actual store where he was going to work, he was sent to the company headquarters in Nishi Shinjuku. One of the floors in the building was all training space. He arrived just before nine. There were three people already seated in the room. He thought there would be more.

There were long folding tables on castors, set up like a classroom. In the front of the room was an electronic whiteboard with a printer attached. The three other people were seated at the back, so my husband went and sat with them. One more person joined them, and immediately after that in walked some people whose smiles and haircuts and clothes told you right away they were the training staff.

The trainers introduced themselves and welcomed the new hires. Then they broke down the training: the next four days will be the first part of the course

where you'll work in a group right here in our training facilities, and for the second part of the course
you'll be at the actual stores where you'll be working
and that on-the-job training will be for three days.
My husband and the other four new hires were then
given a sheet of paper, which listed the year of the
company's founding, number of employees, previous
year's sales, profit overview from the past five years,
the year the company was listed on the Tokyo Stock
Exchange's Second Section, the year it aims to be
bumped up to the Tokyo Stock Exchange's First Section.
The training staff recited everything written on the
paper. Then they showed training videos on customer
service and operating the register. The lights were
lowered for this.

As this was happening more people trickled into
the room, until eventually there were around twenty
people who all must have been new hires.

I try to just lie flat on my back but my body won't
cooperate. One side or the other seems to drift. I'm all
twisted, and it doesn't seem like I'll ever be able to get
back to normal.

I thought my husband would be going to work at
the drugstore from day one. Was the fact that he didn't
tell me what would be happening, even though there
was nothing to hide, was that a quiet little dig at me?

When he came back from the convenience store he had two cans of beer, but neither was for me. He had only planned to buy one can, but once he was in the store decided to get another. He also got a bag of chips. The help-wanted weekly was rolled up and stuck, not very neatly, under one arm.

Now, though, the weekly, full of useless information from a couple weeks back, is lying on the floor about a metre from my head. It wants to curl up, as if it remembers when it was rolled up under his arm. The pages are messy, the edges don't line up neatly, showing the pulp the cloudy white paper is made of.

My husband lay down and fell asleep right where he was, before he even finished his beers. The next morning I picked up the cans and emptied them not in the sink but in the toilet, then took them to the kitchen and rinsed them out and stood them up on the floor to dry. Before he passed out, when he was sitting there drinking his beer and flipping through the weekly, which was only a short while, like fifteen minutes, he had his butt on the vinyl flooring and his legs thrust out in front of him. He was trying to make as little noise as he could, even when he pulled the tab on his beer. But I sat there watching him the whole time, and I really stared, I wasn't trying to hide it. He drank the first can fast, in gulps, and immediately opened the second, even though I later found there was still some left in the first. He stuffed the chips in his mouth by the handful and in no time the bag was empty.

There's an unoccupied stool at the counter at Becker's, to the right of where my husband is slumped over, and on the stool next to it sits a young woman with short hair in a light grey suit. She's been there for a while, looking over every so often at my sleeping husband, looking back to the phone in her hand where she's been typing something.

A newspaper sits on the counter. It's open to the financial page and folded in fourths. There's a pie chart showing the market share of portable music players, under a picture of Sony's new Walkman and the iPod nano that debuted the other day. Whoever folded the newspaper didn't go along with the original creases, and the corners of the squared-up paper look puffy.

When I sent the text to my husband and made his phone buzz, she reacted almost immediately. Her thumbs wiggled in mid-air over her own phone as if still pushing the keys, then she peeled her eyes away from her screen and turned to look at his phone. No one else in the café reacted to his phone buzzing, least of all he, who was asleep. She was sitting a little too far away to make out what it said on his screen. More than likely she was wondering what was up with this passed-out guy who sleeps through his phone buzzing in his face.

He had in his white earbuds. I wonder, if he wasn't listening to his music turned all the way up, would he have woken up to get my message in real time? Even if he did and wrote back, it would just be a chain of the most predictable words, like it was lifted directly from a composition textbook, dry and meaningless.

He has to be at the drugstore in two hours.

The woman slips off her shoes, dangling her stockinged feet from the stool. A few times she reaches down with both hands to massage her calves, which are a little swollen. Her black pumps are on the floor, the left one tipped on its side. The right one is still standing.

After the text came in, she looked for a moment at the earbud nested in his ear. Then she found herself staring intently, considering the ear as a whole. There was a split second when she saw the music seeping out of the space between earbud and ear like a curl of steam or smoke. My husband's hair is cut pretty short, so the ear looked exposed and helpless. All the more so because he doesn't have sideburns, just bare skin.

She stared, but she didn't let herself get lost in the shape of the ear, this fold and that curve, nothing physical like that, instead she focused on the overall impression of a complex object, zoomed out on it, trying to reach the point where the ear stops looking like an ear, even though she knew it was an ear, so as she little by little lost its ear-ness she got the feeling that something unbelievable was happening to her. She stared some more until she just about reached the point of flipping the values of light and shadow in the textures of his ear. She leant her elbow on the counter, then opened her hand like a flower, but almost immediately drew it back to her face, tracing the span between the ear and eye. She decided she would stay there a little longer. But that's as far as she got.

I'm starting to think I should sit up. For a while now I've been feeling it might be more comfortable than lying here. I roll onto my back instead, raise my butt up into the air and bring my knees in towards my face. Then I prop my hips up on my hands and raise my legs straight up in a perfect vertical. I look at my legs, floating against the ceiling. But I can't hold the position for long, no more than ten seconds, then I have to drop my legs back down so they're stretched out flat again.

The earbud cord hanging from my husband's right ear meets up with the cord hanging from his left ear, and the joined cords rest on the counter, brushing up against the sharp pointiness of his bare right elbow resting on the tray. His arm is set at a nearly perfect right angle. The tip of the elbow is covered in marks from old cuts and burns, dark red and purple, that look like stains. After bumping against his right elbow, the cord snakes along the counter to the right, where it reaches the edge of the counter and drops down into the pocket of his jeans. That was where her attention settled, her interest in my husband suddenly fixed on one question: What is he listening to? The music is pumped steadily up the cord into his ears.

The counter is at a window where she can see her reflection and also a view of the café behind her, though the image is not as clear as it would be at night. The tray-return station is reflected in the window too. A staff member comes by every now and again to tidy it up. One is there right now.

The clouds break and let the sun through. Light pours into the café, making anything white-coloured seem to shine and blur at the edges.

The young woman in the grey suit isn't looking at the reflection in the glass now, instead she directs her focus towards what's actually in front of her, beyond the window. That's what she meant to do all along. But it isn't going as she had hoped.

She raises her hips off the stool slightly and touches her face to the glass for a bit, gazing down at the people coming and going in and out of the station. Between the sidewalk and the avenue is a taxi stand with several cars lined up. Just about at the left edge of the window the avenue meets up with a few other roadways, more complicated than a standard four-way intersection. The waiting taxi drivers are leaning back in their seats, reading newspapers or magazines.

There's a pedestrian bridge over the intersection, and the Tokyo Metropolitan Expressway passes over that. From where she sits it looks like the bottom of the highway grazes the walkway below.

My husband's slumped-over upper body expands and recedes with the rhythm of his breathing. The wall immediately to his left is also a window from waist-level up, showing the outside world. Over the ridges of his shoulders and spine she has a direct view of the stairs to the pedestrian bridge. She stares at the people going up and down, at their outfits, at the parasols some are carrying.

A Democratic Party of Japan campaign van is coming up the avenue, blaring its message.

I scrunch up my shoulders and slowly roll my head back, lifting my torso, supporting the weight of my body on the top of my skull. My mouth hangs open.

The guard rails on the pedestrian bridge have a white rust-resistant coating. A kid is pressing his face into the vertical space between two of the bars, peering down at the traffic. The DPJ van passes.

A couple other kids are chasing each other around, chanting *I got you, I go-o-o-ot you* to the tune of "Momotaro's Song", screeching every so often. They're not on the pedestrian bridge, though, they're inside the café. She's looking at my husband again. He's fidgeting a bit, more movement than he's made up until now, which she guesses means he's waking up.

I can see the refrigerator upside down. It seems to be on the verge of taking on human characteristics. It's about to happen, I can see it. But it never quite does. In the end the refrigerator stays a plain old refrigerator.

For some reason I have a recollection of flipping the mattress to find the vinyl flooring wet and covered in mould like green fur.

The high-school boys who had been making noise in the café are now silent, leaning over their mobile phones. One has gone, leaving four.

My husband's neck and shoulders suddenly go slack. It's not clear how this action might be connected to his arm physiologically, but his elbow jerks up into the air and comes crashing back down on the counter. The sound of the impact reverberates through the café. When his elbow strikes the counter she doesn't look towards it, she looks away, back to her own phone for a split second, before returning her gaze to my husband. This is when he wakes up.

My husband, like me, has never managed to make it down to the deepest levels of sleep. To us those levels don't exist. Or they're too far out of our league, something we'll never be able to have, like a hotel suite or first-class seats on a plane. Coming up with the comparison makes me realize how true it is. In his shallow sleep my husband was dreaming that he boarded the train at one of those aerial tracks that a lot of the stations on the Odakyu Line have, but he noticed right away that he was headed in the wrong direction, so he got out at the next stop and went back the way he was supposed to be going, although he wasn't actually sure it was the Odakyu Line he got on, trying to get to his job by 7:30, and although his phone told him it was already 7:23, he was pretty sure he would make it in time.

He reaches for his phone on the tray to find out

what time it actually is. That's when he sees the text I sent him: *Morning! Long night, huh? You okay? Don't push yourself too hard.*

Tears start to flow down his cheeks, more reflex than emotion. There's a warm feeling inside him, but it isn't his own, it's being forced into him from outside. His tears last only a few moments. His head is hazy, to the point that he's mystified by the fact that he feels a connection between who he was when he fell asleep and who he is right now.

He rolls his head around to loosen his neck, which is stiff from sleeping in an awkward position.

I'm on my back again, pointing my chin at the ceiling.

The woman in the grey suit is looking at her phone again, no longer interested in my husband. Over the music in his earbuds he can just make out the receding noise of the speech on the loudspeaker of the DPJ van. It seems like the two sounds have always coexisted, superimposed on one another. Having music playing when he wakes up robs him of the chance to wonder what music he might want to hear, and actually he doesn't even feel like listening to music at all right now, so the song in his ears makes waking up in this less-than-ideal spot for a nap even more of a drag.

When he listens to music with earbuds for a while, it gets to the point where no matter what he's listening to it just sounds like noise pressing on his ear, and he wants to turn it off but he also still wants to be listening to music, and he gets confused about what it is he wants to do. When he was in his early twenties he would put in earplugs instead, the colour of orange and yellow sink sponges. He never knew where he put his earplugs and was always buying new ones. Then he'd find the old ones in his bag or his pockets.

Now he's thirty.

He was sleeping with his glasses on, so now the lenses are smudged with the body oil of his arm. He happens not to be wearing the jeans he always wears, so his lens cloth isn't in his pocket. When he bought the ¥5,900 Zoff glasses, the clerk warned him only to use a lens cloth and not to use napkins like the kind on the tray because they would scratch the lenses, and normally he's careful to do that but this time he has no other option so he takes a napkin and rubs the oiliness off. He puts his glasses back on, then notices the woman in the grey suit sitting at the counter to his right, tapping out a text, and looks at her.

Her body is solid and largish, her froggy eyes bulging, which I would say is his type. The reason

I would say that is because she is me, hair shorter than it is now, when I was half a year into the job at a small advertising-design firm and I would go to Becker's for breakfast. She turns her eyes back to her phone, where she's been typing for some time. I can't read the long passage she's written out. But I know what it says, it's a draft of the longer version of the bland little text I sent before, the real version, not just long but full of love and appreciation for him, with nothing about how tired my body feels, no complaints about whatever weird problems I'm having, just my honest feelings put into words in a long message.

But I can't read the words that are written there.

She looks at him intermittently, which breaks the flow of her writing, and she loses the thread. She erases the whole thing. She gets down off the stool, rights the fallen shoe and wriggles her feet in. Then she steps away. My husband glances over at her large ass. She heads down the stairs. He starts to thumb his phone. Writing a message.

My phone vibrates. Of course it's just a phantom buzz.

At that moment I register movement in the kitchen. Almost immediately I see it: an unusually large cockroach.

She leaves Becker's, but instead of going to the office she goes back to the station. The Sobu Line headed for Shinjuku arrives almost immediately. Until a little past Ichigaya the track runs along the green water of the outer moat. The far bank is a grassy slope with trees planted at regular intervals, and partway up the slope it becomes a stone wall, the top of which runs beside the road above. Many of the buildings along the road have signs saying they're print shops and tutoring centres.

I throw my phone at the cockroach, even though there's no way I'll ever hit it. The cover slides off and the battery pops out, still held by the battery ribbon.

The cockroach is unhurt, of course. It scuttles up the face of the fridge, past the lower compartment and almost to the middle of the upper compartment, when it stops. I bet it was the roach that knocked over the beer cans.

I get up from the futon, wanting to kill the cockroach. I grab the help-wanted weekly off the floor and roll it up tightly, back into the tube it once was. The roach darts from the fridge to the wall, scurrying along near the ceiling into the room where I was lying. The grey suit is in a cabinet in the room, the hardest one to reach by far which is fine because all we have in there are things we never take out, old letters, my husband's old game consoles and cartridges, my work from art school, my grey suit which I didn't bother to hang on a hanger but is at least in the plastic bag it came in, I think. I'm pretty sure the suit is stuffed in there. By now it's probably covered in mould. The cockroach slips into the drawer.

JAPANESE FICTION
FROM PUSHKIN PRESS

RECORD OF A NIGHT TOO BRIEF

Hiromi Kawakami

Translated by Lucy North

SPRING GARDEN

Tomoka Shibasaki

Translated by Polly Barton

SLOW BOAT

Hideo Furukawa

Translated by David Boyd

Ms ICE SANDWICH

Mieko Kawakami

Translated by Louise Heal Kawai

THE BEAR AND THE PAVING STONE

Toshiyuki Horie

Translated by Geraint Howells

THE END OF THE MOMENT WE HAD

Toshiki Okada

Translated by Sam Malissa